Vacations Can Be Fatal
three novellas
A Vacation to Die For
A Vacation in Hell
A Very Scenic Trap

Contents

Tammy Sheridan, a Valley Girl, like, you know, those in the eighties, won a vacation to die for in a contest. First stop was Cancun, second stop, Managua, third stop, Bocas del Toro, forth stop, Cartagena, fifth stop, Rio de Janiero.

She didn't make the fifth stop.

Tammy was considered a little weird, but was liked. No one had any reason to kill her. Somebody did.

Max Reede was warned about going to Hell Island, particularly about El Diablo Mountain. He said he always found these kinds of places were just stories to scare gullible people. It would be a cheap two weeks in a place that wasn't overrun with tourists. Voodoo and Hoodoo were just silly superstitions. He doesn't have a superstitious bone in his body. – Then how do you explain this?

Nancy Ann Gilders had married Harry Silvers after knowing him only eleven days. He was very wealthy, she was comfortable, but not rich.

They spent four years in a very happy marriage. They traveled to many places.

Then he was murdered with a very rare and hard-to-trace poison. He left a daughter and son and Nancy Ann.

All three had apparently been cleared in the murder. All three became very personally wealthy at his death.

Nancy Ann had to get away. She made plans with the daughter to take a trip.

Then it got scary. Was someone trying to get rid of all three heirs?

About the author

CD began writing fiction in 1984 and has more than 300 books published as of 3/15/16 in SciFi, murder, orchid culture and various other fields.

He now resides Gualaca, Chiriqui, Panamá, where he continues research into epiphytic plants and plays music with friends. He loves the culture of the indigenous people and counts a majority of his closer friends among that group. He funds those he can afford through the universities where they have all excelled. "The Indios are very intelligent people, they are simply too poor (in material things and money.) to pursue higher education."

CD loves Panamá and the people, despite horrendous experiences (Free e-book; *Fading Paradise*). He plans to spend the rest of his life in the paradise that is Panamá

CD is involved in research of natural cancer cure at this time. It has proven effective in all cases, so far. It is based on a plant that has been in use for thousands of years, is safe, available, and cheap. He was cured of a serious lymphoma with use of the plant, *Ambrosia peruviana.*

Information about this cure is free on the FaceBook page Ambrosia peruviana for cancer. CD asks only that all who try it please report on its effectiveness on that group.

Clint Faraday
book 55
A Vacation to Die For
© 2019 by C. D. Moulton

Contents

Valley Girl Vacation

Tammy Fordham Sheridan answered her pink custom-designed Blackberry. It was a bad time for chat, but only her very closest few friends had the number.

"Tammy? Wow, girlfriend! You won!" Leslee Albins cried.

"I did? Like, what?"

"The vacation! You remember! It was, like, late last Saturday night when we were, like, in Cosmosation! You bought that ticket from Eddie Baines. One of those things that, like, cure AIDS or whatever. You know."

"Beddie Edie? I, like, maybe, remember giving him ten dollars for something.

"A vacation?"

"It's that, like, some charity smuggin thing, A Vacation to Die For. Your name won. You go to five, like, special exotic ports, all paid and a hundred dollars a day for, like, things."

"Well, what ports? I don't ... but it might be, like, exotic en fin."

"Let's see. Cancún – I was there. Clicking at dusk til. Managua. Big night club sort of thing, like. Bocas del Toro? I never ... it's that place like Key West! Sher can inform. Was. With Phil and that Arturo hood. Last year. Very surfy. Cartagena. Sort of, like vacationy, family shit, you know? Change. Rio. You liked Rio. It ends there at, like, that Mardi Gras or whatever kinda thing. First class acommodos all the way.

"Fly out of LAX Monday! Like, get your ass in motion, girl! Enjoy!"

"Oh, well. Might. Dregsville around here."

They chatted. Tammy decided she wouldn't go, then changed her mind. She could always come back if it was dullsville or whatever. She liked the Latin guys. The ones who didn't think they owned you. Not the macho facade. She could live without that, like, crap. Arturo Finch turned out to be like that, but some of Sherri's friends were, like, gross!

Bocas del Toro. Panamá. That place where her sister, Sherri, said that Indian was the best she every laid. Guillermo, that was it. She would look him up. Sherri had good taste in men.

This might be fun! She did like to get away from the same old same old all the time. Lately, life was, like, b-o-r-r-i-n-g-g.

She could try some of those things she bought to wear to parties and never did. Let loose on a vacation. Why have super boobs if you don't, like, flaunt them?

Cancún was Cancún. She'd been there. It was fun, but three nights was, like, one too many. Managua was different than she expected. She would have liked it if she were a guy. Lots of hookers and everything was cheap.

She flew into Bocas Town on Isla Colón at four thirty on Monday. This place had better be better than Managua, but it would have to be if Sherri liked it.

She got off the plane and stretched. It wasn't the kind of flight she would prefer, but she could understand that the island wasn't big enough for a proper airport where the big jets could land.

She went to baggage. Sherri had been right about the Indians. She could just die for skin like that! She wanted to touch the men. Sherri said their skin really was like soft satin! It sure looked it! That black hair and the sexy eyes that looked ready for bed! Sherri said they kept the promise!

Oh, that one was pure, like, *gorgeous*! He looked at her and smiled with the most perfect teeth she ever saw!

"Can I help you with your luggage or to find your hotel?"
God! Thank you Jesus! He speaks English!
"I, like, would ... yes. Thanks. I'm Tammy."
"Guillermo. Do you have a hotel reservation, Tammy?"
"Oh, like certain, you know. Tropical Suites."
"Very nice. You'll like it. Deck on the water and all that. Famous people stay there. Are you one?"
"A people? Yes. Famous, I wish!"
"I think you'll be fun. California?"
"Uh-huh. It's that, like, obvious?"
"Like, fer shur!" He laughed. She couldn't help laughing herself.

He took her to the hotel and helped her find her room. She just couldn't stop herself from touching his arm. The skin really was as satiny as Sherri said! This was the prize stud! The very same identical one! She didn't like the idea of seconds to her own sister, like, but this was a, like, special kind of thing!

"I think you met my younger sister a year or so ago? Sherri Sheridan?"

"Sherri? Ah, yes! You look like her, some. You're better looking, but please don't tell her I said so."

They laughed. "Are you free for dinner?" she asked.

"I'm not free for anything. There aren't many ways for a man to make a living here. I try to be honest with people. I'm a whore."

"How, like, refreshing! Most men are, but not many admit it!

"I have, like, oodles of money, and this trip is paid for, so what time will I pick you up?"

"You already did!"

She loved it! He was for a good time and this was his living.

She ran her hand down his arm. He pulled her close and kissed her. It was the sexiest kiss she could remember! Like, bazookas! She'd bet the farm he made a damned good living! She'd bet the farm he was as good in bed as Sherri said!

She said she'd be ready about seven if that was suitable?

He would be there. She would find he wasn't an expensive date and that he knew all the best places – besides the ones on her.

As soon as he left she got out her phone. It rang three times at the number she punched on the speed dial.

"Hello? Tammy?" Leslee answered.

"My god! This really is a vacation to die for! That guy Sherri told us about, you know, the Indian? Guillermo?

"I met him! He's going to dinner with me and we're going to have the best night of my life! He's, like, *gorgeous*! And he's out front that he's, like, a whore.

"I never could understand why a man would pay a whore before! Now I know, like, fer shur! God, he's beautiful! And, like, he's honest and fun and I got lost in his eyes and I'm like a virgin right now! God! I'm so scared I won't, like, measure up, you know?"

"Girl, if he's like Sherri said, I'm so jealous I could, like, strangle you! Really? I mean, *really*?"

"Really real real, Girlfriend! Picture time! I'll bet he won't blink if I, like, want him naked!

"God, do I want him naked!"

They laughed. Tammy rang off and went to the shower. She was going to look better than she ever had before! This was going to be the best night of her life!

She was, like, fifty miles from being a virgin, but she was as nervous as one. He was to *die* for!

Tammy snuggled even closer, if that was even possible, to Guillermo. The night had been even more fantasmagoric than she'd fantasized!

He was, like, a god! It wasn't possible for a mere human being to be even half that good! Or that handsome. Or that open.

He had taken her to several places for the native foods and for fun in the native bars. She thought she would have to spend a thousand dollars, but the whole night was less than fifty!

He knew everybody. It was obvious that he had been to bed with all those sexy women. She wouldn't be surprised if he'd been to bed with more than a few of the men – the Indios (they called the native people Indios here). They all hugged him like it.

Well, they were a touching people. They all hugged her when he introduced them. A whole body hug. Tight, like, and it was only partly because she was a gringa and sorta blond. They seemed to be, like, really affectionate with each other as well as with her.

Sherri said they looked at things different. Maybe they just touched a lot.

She was about to, like, slide out of the bed, but Guillermo woke up and pulled her to him. She said she had to use the bathroom, so he went with her. They got in the shower and she did things she never thought she'd do. Ever. She loved every picosecond of it!

They went to breakfast at a place called Don Chicho's, though that wasn't the name on it. It was the only place open that early.

That early? She never ever got up before nine thirty! It was only seven!

She couldn't remember ever feeling so very damned *good*!

Guillermo had to go to Isla San Cristóbal. He would be back by five. She would take the bus to Boca del Drago and be back for him.

She never got back.

Calling Clint Faraday

"Clint? Sergio here, in Bocas. Are you on the comarca?"

"On the way to Chiriqui Grande. Why?"

"I have a murder that I can't figure. It's not the type of thing that anyone here would do because she didn't know anyone here before last night. Guillermo spent the night with her and said she was sort of flaky, but really a good person."

"Why me?"

"She was from California. Guillermo said he was with her sister a little over a year ago. Everyone with them called the sister a Valley Girl. She was very much like her sister.

"Clint, if there was even a small hint that anyone here would kill her, I can't find it. You're the only one I know who might make something of the mess."

"Okay. I'm a little bored with perfection at the moment. I'll run over there and see what I can find. You know the important things."

"Yes. First thing was to secure her room and the safety box in her name even before they brought her back from Drago. That's where she was killed. She was strangled with a piece of polypropylene rope."

"No more than ninety five percent of the people here have that laying around. Should be easy!"

"Picture a fist with the middle finger erect!"

Clint called his wife, Tyna, to say there was another murder on Isla Colón. He didn't know when he'd get back.

"Hmm. The Darien, east, then Bocas, west. Can't say you don't cover the whole country!

"Get rice and flour for Mom while you're in Bocas."

Clint went past Chiriqui Grande and on to the islands. He

docked at his deck in his house on the island and talked a few minutes with Janet Storie. Her husband, Nick Storie had met Clint and family and once stayed with them on the comarca. Nick had a place on Martinique, but preferred Bocas. The people were a lot easier to get along with here. Nick was with Judi Lum, Clint's neighbor there in Bocas Town, visiting with a big gangster from the states or some such thing. Nick knew the biggest of the big.

Clint remembered his invitation for them to stay there. They took care of the place. He almost never spent time there anymore. Janet said Cole and Nicole (her daughter was Nicole, as was Clint's) were off to Drago to surf.

"I wish I'd remembered you were here! Nick could help Sergio with the murder!"

Janet laughed. "Another working vacation! No thanks!"

He chatted awhile, then went to the police station where his old friend, chief of violent crimes there, met him. They went to a new restaurant for lunch. Sergio filled him in with what they knew.

She was from California. She had won some kind of dream vacation. This was the forth stop. She didn't know anyone here. She spent the night with their good friend, Guillermo. She went to Drago on the bus. She was found four hours later by some mangroves near the beach. She was strangled with a piece of half inch polypropylene rope. Black. Her room at the Suites was sealed immediately, as was her safe box. Dr. Arrends had the body at the morgue. She had a sister, who had been notified. She was in Modesto, California, and would be there on the morning flight from PMA.

They talked about other things, then went to the Suites to carefully search her room. They got the things from the locked box: passport, ticket to Cartagena and another to Rio.

Two hundred fifty thousand dollar insurance policy made out to her sister. Some fine jewelry.

There was nothing. She kept a diary, but Clint saw little new there. It was almost boring.

He read the last page, a short note or two: *Flew in Bocas and met Sherri's 'Oh, Wow!' Guillermo. He really real real __is__!!!! Tonight with him!!!!!*

Surfers just like Pismo & SD. Same ones. Borrrring!

"I wonder if she meant that literally?" Clint asked of no one.

"What?" From Sergio.

"Same ones."

"You don't make sense. You seldom do."

They finished and headed for the station. They'd have to wait for the sister to know if there was anything else to hang onto this. It was going to be a hard case no matter what. The two hardest kinds of cases were when a lot of people had a motive or when no one seemed to have one.

Sherri Sheridan got off the flight with a rather handsome sort. Surfer type. She was pretty, but not quite to the standard of her sister if the photos were accurate. Clint had talked with Guillermo for awhile, waiting for the flight to land. Guillermo would remember Sherri.

He did. He went to hug her and say he was very sorry they had to meet again under these circumstances. Tammy had seemed to be a special kind of person. She reminded him of her little sister the minute he saw her.

She introduced Eddie Baines, the person who had sold her sister the ticket that won the vacation. He said it was just some charity thing his buddy, Phil Vanderhaven, was selling to help with an AIDS hospice they were building in LA. All the group bought a ticket. They did that kind of thing for their friends. Everybody was well-off enough that it didn't hurt. If they wanted a vacation, they took it. This was a lark. They usually didn't even know who won anything. This was the first time they had anyone in their little group win anything, not that it mattered.

"It was a vacation to die for," Eddie said.

"Then she met Guillermo and told Les he was to die for, then she.... Oh, God!" Sherri cried. "The sherif said she was murdered? I can't believe it! No one would, like, kill Tammy! Everybody liked her!"

"Phil will be all to pieces. He sold the tickets, really. He was kind of, like, wanting to get a, like, more permanent relation-ship with her," Eddie said. "He couldn't make up his mind if he would, like, marry her or you!"

"Oh, Phil's, like, too emotional. Date you a few times and think he was in love. He's a nice enough guy, and, like, a maybe," Sherri replied. "I'm not ready for that thing yet.

"This isn't what we're here for. Like, ... I've gotta quit saying that. It's how we talk at home.

"Where do we go? What do we do?"

"She was staying at the Tropical Suites," Sergio answered. "We can take your things there, then we can try to find some kind of reason for this. She didn't know anyone here except for Guillermo for one night. We can't find a trace of motive or a suspect."

"We'll take my boat to Drago as soon as you're ready," Clint suggested. "She was killed there. Maybe you'll spot someone. She must have. Someone who's not supposed to be here or who had motive from California."

They agreed to that. It was a starting place. They didn't have one until now.

Sergio took them to the Suites while Clint went to get his

boat. He picked them up at the dock at the Suites and they headed for Boca del Drago and the surfer crowd.

Clint was still considering the diary and the notation that they were the same surfers. Did she mean it literally? Did she know any of them personally? Was it simply a generic statement?

That had to be cleared up. Clint particularly wanted to know if anyone had unexpectedly checked out yesterday or this morning. That could prove very telling.

They chatted about California on the way. It seemed they were a little clique of friends who were stuck back in the time of the valley girls, fifteen years ago. It reminded Clint of people he knew who were still in the hippie era. There were quite a few of those in Panamá.

The ride was pleasant. There was a slight chop, but nothing to affect Clint's boat. He came into the bay side to avoid the waves on the Caribbean side and docked at the hotel dock there. They got out and Sherri suggested they go to the hotel restaurant. She hadn't eaten anything since she got up.

They ordered a light late lunch and watched the people. Clint asked Vanda, their waitress, if she'd noted Tammy.

"The dead girl? I think she was in here with a surfer. Blond and kind of handsome. I couldn't identify him. He was just a gringo surfer. They tend to look alike after awhile. They're not interested in me except as a waitress. I'm not interested in them except as clients. If he came in here a few more times, I'd remember, because that means tips."

"Tammy was a surfer. I'm not very good at it," Sherri said. "Eddie doesn't do much, but he's kind of, like – I promised not to talk like that!

"Tammy would know surfers from almost everywhere. She had the same psych kind of way about her. She was popular.

She probably just met someone she'd seen before, but that could mean anything or nothing. I know she was always saying she met someone or other from Hawaii or Australia or whatever back home."

"I think that girl with the long black hair is from Hawaii," Eddie said. "Her name's ... Sydney Lindy or Sydney Lindsay. I met her in SD on the beach. A competition sort of thing. She's from Australia.

"Say! Maybe she saw Tammy here!"

"Find out!" Sergio ordered. Eddie got up and went to a slender pretty girl and talked for a bit, then came back to say she had seen Tammy on the beach when she got off the bus, but she was with Hilo Hank and had just waved. She was talking with some girl from the bus. A native by the looks of her.

Clint told Sergio to wander around with the two to see if they spotted anyone else. He had to use his computer for a few things. He had an idea.

"Where are all the surfers from?"

"And did any leave yesterday or this morning. I also want to investigate some other things. Something doesn't fit here. I can't see what it is, but someone said something...."

"One of those things that nag, but you don't know what or why?"

"Exactly! Surfers travel with names like Hawaii Hank. Most of them haven't got a clue as to real names."

"So! California Carl or San Diego Sam might be here?"

"Uh-huh. Also note that Sherri and Eddie look like typical surfers. She isn't and he's just under the wire. We might be looking for a surfer who isn't."

"Isn't a surfer. You don't get me this time!"

"I'm going to spend some time trying to find the worm in

this barrel of apples."

"Knock it off! I'll talk later. Maybe we can spot someone. There's one thing that will give the one not a surfer away, I think."

Clint nodded. The surfers were all tanned. He'd seen two already who weren't tanned, but they didn't look like surfers either. Someone with a surfer handle and no tan would be a good bet to be a phony if not the one they wanted.

Computer Legwork

Clint soon got a good connection. He went to surfer sites and searched for Hilo Hank, who was Henry Francis Goode. He won a minor competition. San Diego. June 12, 2011.

He had the places Tammy had been outside the US from her passport. She had been in France in June and early July, 2011. Unless she knew him from somewhere else he wasn't who they were after.

Sydney Lindsay was Lorraine Lindsay. Sergio would get her passport information – as well as everyone else there.

Eddie Baines was Edward Louis Baines.

He checked on the raffle where Tammy won the vacation. Unless it was just one of those things a local club had, it wasn't registered.

He thought. He checked hospices for AIDS patients in Southern California. There were several. None of them had run a raffle.

This wasn't accomplishing much.

He had another idea. He got the airline ticket numbers from the stubs and unused tickets Tammy had. He went to the police net and asked for full information about the ticket purchases.

They were all bought for cash. Paul Vance made the purchases. They were purchased four days before the supposed raffle win. They were for Tammy Fordham Sheridan – with her passport number for boarding pass issue.

Paul Vance. Thirty four of them. None of whom seemed likely.

She had a draw of a hundred dollars a day. From an ATM card.

He checked the account. Opened by a Peter Vincent.

The killer's initials were P. V.

Was there a ... yes. Eddie had mentioned Phil Vanderhaven, who had set up the raffle and who wanted to marry Tammy. Had he arranged this to ask her to marry him, she laughed in his face or something, he killed her?

Very thin. He wasn't decided if it was her or Sherri he wanted. There could have been others. He would have to do a lot of digging on this one.

Panamá tourists in Bocas del Toro with the initials P. V. He checked immigration. Ponci Vaninni, Italy. Patrick Varness, Ireland. Phryne Velson, Norway.

Vanderhaven was Dutch. Norway wasn't that far. Velson was staying at the Bahia in Bocas Town. Vaninni was at the Sagitario. Varness was with friends in The Bluffs.

Were any of them surfers?

Phryne had brought a board with him.

Clint checked the surfer websites for him. A small line that he was third in a competition in Australia last year. Nothing else.

He called the Bahia. Velson was scheduled to go to Las Tablas. He had taken the early water taxi for Almirante.

He would have time to get to David ... no. Santiago if he took the Panamá City bus. He would go to Las Tablas from Santiago.

Police net: He had taken the bus to Santiago. It had arrived there less than an hour ago. He was on it.

Santiago to Las Tablas ... there would be no checkpoint. He could disappear easily enough. The problem remaining was that he would have to use that passport to get out of the country.

Or to register in a hotel. Clint had an alert for use of the passport.

He might be a lot smarter to go to Las Tablas and disappear from there. It would be a bit too suspicious for him to not get there. Even people with several legal passports had records. If this one wasn't legal, there would be no registration from Norway.

There could be. A trace for a legal alias was in order.

Clint thought, then called Pedro Placido, the helicopter pilot he used. He said to pick him up in Bocas as soon as possible. Las Tablas.

Clint got off the chopper and said to wait a little while. He may be right back.

Velson was supposed to be at the Big Beach Hotel, just west of Las Tablas. Pedro said he could land on the beach there so they went to land down from the hotel. Clint went inside to meet Velson, who had checked in less than an hour before.

Velson was a dark-haired light complexioned man in his thirties. The passport information came in just before Clint went into the hotel so he already knew Velson wasn't his man. His only passport had been used for France, New Zealand, Thailand and Australia. This was his first trip to this side of the Earth.

Velson was a slender, slightly scruffy man with a Van Dyke beard. He spoke passable English. He had never been to California and didn't want to go there. He might want to go to Hawaii some day. The Heineken beer here was nothing like in Europe.

That was it. Clint headed back for Bocas Town.

Sergio said Ponci Vaninni was Ponci Vaninni. Sherri and Eddie said they saw three people they knew from elsewhere, surfers. Sergio had checked them out and found they weren't any part of anything to do with the murder, though he would keep an eye on one of them. Vincent Porter. There was something a little phony about him.

"He was just a little too stoned," Sherri said. "You could smell the pot in his hair when you got close. Tammy taught me how to do that because it could mean the guy was in some dream world and you couldn't really trust what he said, much of the time."

"Well, that's ... Sherri, do you have a picture of Phil Vanderhaven?"

"Phil? I think so." She rummaged around in her bag and got a small picture album out. There were twenty or so photos of people, mostly in groups at nightclubs or such. A few were single subjects. Vanderhaven was one.

Phil Vanderhaven was a handsome slender man, about twenty five years old. The picture wasn't very clear, but should be enough.

"Sergio, you can...."

"... see if he's here."

Clint grinned.

"Phil? Why would he...?" Eddie asked.

"Because there was no contest. Tammy was registered for the flights and at the hotels four days before the supposed drawing for the non-existent raffle.

"I think you'll find he's staying at The Bluffs with some friends, according to the information immigration has."

"Eddie, Sherri? Will you circulate and see if anyone's seen him here? Clint and I will go to The Bluffs to see if maybe he's really got friends there," Sergio suggested. Eddie and Sherri agreed.

Clint and Sergio took the police truck to The Bluffs and

went to the house of the supposed friends of Vanderhaven. He was there. He wasn't Vanderhaven. He was a very Irish man with red hair and intense blue eyes and an open friendly personality. He wasn't a surfer type. He was there to write articles for the surfer and tourists magazines. He was more into the backpackers than the surfers.

"Shit! We're back to square zero!" Sergio complained on the way back to Drago. "We can't even get to square one from here!"

"Ain't it the truth! I had it all figured for him. We would have a celebration about how smart and clever I am tonight, then I'd go back to Cusapín and brag about it! As you said, 'Shit!' This gets us less than nowhere."

They parked and went into the restaurant for a beer. It was just before dusk and they were tired and disappointed.

Eddie came in about fifteen minutes later to announce, "You were right, I think! Phil was here. Some people saw him at the Mondo Taitu last night. In Bocas Town.

"They weren't sure, but the picture looked a lot like him. The picture's two years old, but he looks a lot like that. His hair's not so long now is all.

"We met Irene Fletcher and her latest. We met in Oahu last year. Is it okay for Sherri and me to stay here tonight?"

"They're the ones who saw Vanderhaven in Bocas Town?" Sergio asked.

"No. That was the German girls, Helen and Gretta. Phil bought them a drink. He dropped a line that he uses, but a lot of surfers use that one. 'Weren't you in Sydney or Hawaii or whatever last June?' kind of thing. They say no, and you say they had to be. There couldn't be two girls that beautiful in only one world. Crap line, you know."

"You can stay. It may be better if he doesn't see you quite

yet – if he's still here," Sergio replied. "One victim's one too many!"

Clint and Sergio got into Clint's boat and headed back to Bocas Town. It had been a long day.

"Mondo Taitu?" Sergio asked.

"About nine. Nobody much around before. Maybe Barco later if he's not there. He's probably long gone. I wish Eddie'd gotten the name he's using!"

"Ha! Not the way this one's going. He's got phenomenal luck on his side!"

"Yes. I'll go rest for a couple of hours. Meet at Mondo at nine?"

"Uh-huh."

Clint dropped Sergio at the police dock and went to his place. Judi Lum, his neighbor, was sitting on his deck with Janet and Nick Storie. They caught up on what was going on back in Florida. Nick was now the head of violent crimes in Naples. His son was in Gainesville University, studying computer science. He had already made a couple of inventions and was getting very wealthy. His daughter, Nicole, was studying criminal procedures and forensics sciences.

Clint discussed his case with Nick, who said he was probably right about the killer, but it could be contracted. Surely, Vanderhaven wouldn't be stupid enough to be there in Bocas.

"I have to find motive!" Clint said. "There doesn't seem to be any. Tammy wasn't into blackmail – which there's no evidence of anyhow. He was trying to get either Sherri or Tammy to marry him. He would not ...."

"Hey, stupid!" Judi cried. "Check on his finances! You said that the Sheridan sisters are disgustingly rich! Maybe he's not as rich as he would like everyone to think?"

"But ... why kill her, even if she did turn him down in a nasty way – which wouldn't suit her personality."

"Would the sister marry him?"

"Sherri? She said he's a solid maybe. So did Tammy."

"So Sherri will get all the money, not just half? What do their parents have to say about it?"

"According to my information they're dead. That plane crash out of Lourdes six years ago."

"Get a copy of that will!" Nick demanded. "There may be a lot more to this ... I have a friend who can get that in a flash. You met Pancho. He even came back to stay with you a time or two."

Judi smirked and took out her cell phone. "Manny? Judi.

"Listen. We need to know what the will ... here's Clint."

"Manny? Hi! I just got back from Drago. A girl was murdered there. Tammy Sheridan. Her sister's here. We need to know what the will said that left the girls Midas rich.

"I'll e-mail the info. Five minutes."

He chatted a few minutes, then went to his computer to send Manny Matthews (Actually Marko Bocinni, retired mafia boss from the states) what information Sergio had supplied about the parents. He then spent about half an hour chatting with Judi and the Stories. Ben and Earl, gay neighbor couple, came to fix a quick gourmet meal. Just before Clint headed for the Mondo Taitu and Sergio, Manny sent the information.

Clint read over the sheet and sighed. This was something that gave whoever married Sherri a motive and a half!

<u>*Where There's a Will...*</u>

"I'll tell you what I think after we find this guy, but it won't be Vanderhaven unless he's a total abject idiot. I have to find a lot about Vanderhaven. I really do!"

"Such as?"

"Such as ... wait until you see what the will said."

"Will? You're back to not making any sense. Tammy left a will?"

"Not that I know of. Her parents did."

They went in. After a few conversations they found several people who saw someone who looked a lot like the picture. He was called Artie. He was from Texas. He was okay if a little crude. Some surfers were, but he seemed more a phony than a real surfer.

Clint asked if he was staying somewhere they knew about. They said the Grand Kahuna, but he was probably already gone. He was in two nights ago. He also went to the Barco Hundido.

They went to the Grand Kahuna. Arthur Finch had stayed there two nights and had gone back to Texas yesterday. Yveth, the girl watching the place, said he was a sort of demanding type. He was more like some of the older gringos. He didn't ask for things, he ordered them.

He looked a lot like the picture, but sort of different. The picture looked like a nice enough guy, this one wasn't. This one seemed not to even know his own name. She had called him twice and he hadn't even looked up, then had suddenly said he wasn't listening and what did she want. Once she heard him make a call on his roaming. He was right by the door and didn't know she was inside. He said it was Phil calling.

Clint thought a bit, then said they should go to the station. He wanted to know what kind of information immigration had on Arthur Finch.

"He'll be Vanderhaven?"

"No way! He wants people to think he was. That was a bit too contrived. This whole mess is! Something is off kilter! Badly off kilter!

"I want you to read what the parents' will said. I want to know exactly who Finch is. Everyone says he's a hood type."

Clint called Manny and explained he had to know what connections Arthur Finch had to whoever.

"Finch? Arturo Finchesi? I think he had the name changed legally. He wants to get away from Papa's rep. He's another pea. Papa was into some things in Houston, Texas, and was branching out. We stopped most of it in California, but he's got irons in that fire."

"Hired goon type?"

"Not for money. He's got more than enough. Favors, maybe. Maybe a hit as a lark. He's a killer type like his Pops. Maybe to keep anyone in his new circle from finding out what he really is. He has pretensions."

"So he might be here to kill someone as a favor or because it would stop him from being identified as being what he is?"

There was a pause. "And you wanted a copy of that will. Someone has used or pressured him to kill the girl. The Vanderhaven person."

"I don't think so. I really don't. Someone's trying to make it look like Vanderhaven had it done or did it himself. Question is: Who?"

"Careful, Clint! Could be a double take! Check on exactly where Vanderhaven really is ... I'll do that!"

"This thing was thought out almost all the way. I'm not jumping to anymore conclusions. I think I've been wrong all along. About a lot of things." He and Sergio went to the station where Clint handed Sergio his outline of the will.

Standard opening.

First party: Allen Frederick Sheridan

To my wife, Arlene Fordham Sheridan, all possessions to be disbursed at her discretion. Should she predecease me, all possessions except exceptions on codicil are to be placed into the charge of my oldest daughter, Tammy Fordham Sheridan for disbursement as she deems fit. Should she predecease me such items are to be tendered to my younger daughter, Sherri Fordham Sheridan.

amend: Two millions of dollars cash are to be first awarded to my younger daughter, Sherri Fordham Sheridan.

Second party: Arlene Fordham Sheridan

Presented as afore stated with the names of Allen Frederick Sheridan and Arlene Fordham Sheridan reversed in position.

"Hmm. So Sherri gets the whole kit and kaboodle now," Sergio commented. "Whoever marries her gets the brass ring."

Clint handed him the list of assets. "It's a platinum ring."

Cash in held accounts: May 1, 2008:

HSBC: $24,894,640.71

1st Federal S&L: $11,673,458.20

Chase: $43,728,977.76

"Eighty million dollars, *in cash*?! Why in unholy Hell would she take a vacation won in a contest?!"

"She was a Valley Girl. It was a smuggin lark, like."

"Sheesh!"

"So. Where is Vanderhaven and who's really behind it?"

"Who's your candidate? This Finch hood?"

"For the actual killing, probably. I want to know who set it up. It could be Vanderhaven, but he's on the back burner for the moment. It could be Baines. He sold the phony ticket. It could be Sherri, but that would seem excessive unless there's something we don't know. It could be from something we don't know diddly about.

"I want to check on a few things. Her lawyer would handle them. Do you have a way to contact her lawyer?"

"It will be on the form. We had to send them a copy of the death certificate."

Clint looked them up. Kline, Donalds, Levin, Murray, Mendez & Associates. There was a phone number. He called.

"I'm with the police in Panamá. A client of your firm, Miss Tammy Fordham Sheridan, was murdered by strangulation here two days ago. I must speak with the person in charge of her account with you. Investigation necessitates further information. You are guaranteed full security of non-disclosure."

"Yes. I heard about that. Tammy was a very nice person. I believe Dan Miller handles the family's legal matters. One moment, please?"

"Dan Miller?"

She laughed. "Yes. There are seven unlisted associates.

"Dan? This is a police officer in Panamá. About Tammy? Can you spare a few minutes of your valuable time?"

"Thanks, Cindy. I have nothing to do for the next hour or two, but don't tell him that!"

"Oops! He's on the line!"

They both laughed. "I'm Dan. Dan Miller. How can I help you? Tammy was a friend as well as a client. Sort of flaky and sort of fun."

"Clint Faraday. I'm an investigator. This case is weird and complicated. I have to know about anyone who she had any legal dealings with. I have to know if she has a will, particularly one that no one knew about."

"I see. She might still be alive if someone knew about it?"

"It's a distinct possibility. It would be a matter of how it was worded."

"Oh?"

"Was there a clause that would limit what the spouse of the sister could get for a certain time?"

"I see. I think I know where this is going. The parents' will left everything solely in Tammy's charge. Someone wants to get their hands on more than the two million Sherri has, so kills Tammy, then marries Sherri.

"I've checked on the financial situations of several of the people at Tammy's insistence. Might I have checked on the one who killed her?"

"Or hired her murder."

"I see. Finch has a few million, but it is from gangster connections of the father. He isn't the type who has exhibited any desire for more. He is disposed to violence.

"Baines is very comfortable. He seems a real person. It is my understanding he is there with Sherri.

"Leslee – I haven't a clue as to why she had Leslee Annemarie Albins checked – is more than comfortable. She is what we refer to as Valley Girls, but, then, so is Sherri and so was Tammy.

"Phillip Vanderhaven is comfortable, but has some small financial problems. He doesn't seem concerned with money. He has the ability, proven, to get as much money as he wants. He is a very talented sculptor whose art garners as much as half a million a shot – and he's got a short waiting list.

"He's somewhat bisexual. It's not a problem here, though it may seem that it would be to someone not from Southern

California. Panamá is not Southern California."

"It's almost part of the culture here. Nobody cares. I doubt Tammy was the type to try to blackmail anyone. My own fourteen year old son tells me about his new experiences, which would *not* happen there. I try not to react like the gringo I was. I act like it's, 'Oh, really? Did you enjoy it?' It's not how I feel I can tell you!"

"If she knew anything about anyone, she would giggle and joke about it with them and would probably tell them something about herself. I feel your son is like that?"

"Yes. He's Indio. They like sex and like to talk and joke about it.

"I guess you can't shorten my suspect list?"

"You asked about a will? I haven't answered specifically?"

"Oh? What?"

"Sherri is going to get the shock of finding she doesn't get anything but the big house here. She already has two million dollars she hasn't spent a nickel of. The house and grounds are on the order of five million more. She'll probably sell that to avoid the taxes. Sherri's would-be will learn that also. Had it been known would Tammy still be alive?"

"Very, very probably. Thanks. Who or what gets the eighty million plus?"

"Six relatives on her mother's side and four on her father's. They are all ordinary middle class people who deserve it. Tammy was like that. There are several other relatives who don't deserve the time of day and won't be getting it. She always said that a person who didn't try to improve himself and his family wasn't going to be enabled at being a bum! Not by her!"

"I think I would have liked Tammy. I tend to like Sherri and I do like Baines. I do not like Finch, though I've never met him.

"He was here, you know. He left yesterday. We didn't know about him then or he would be sitting in a cell right now."

"He killed her?"

"I'd say so. I want to know who and why."

"Yes. He had no personal motive. I will aid you in any way I can. Feel free to call on me at anytime.

"I really do have a client waiting."

"Thanks again. You've helped a lot in certain areas." He hung up.

"You said a few things?" Sergio asked.

"Sherri doesn't get the millions. A few relatives do. Sherri gets her two million and the house, which is five million more. She won't be able to afford the taxes, so will sell it.

"Finch is the son of a mobster and is a violence freak and a hood, as we suspected.

"Vanderhaven can get half a million for a sculpture. He has a waiting list. He isn't into money. He's – please don't let it bother you – a bit bisexual."

"That's what the bit about Nito was. Who cares?"

"Leslee was checked. He doesn't know why."

"I don't either, not to mention I don't know from nothing who the hell Leslee is."

"I don't either. Tammy must have had a reason to have her checked. They're all a long way from hurting for money or anything else. There has to be something else behind it. Nobody had motive."

"Nobody we know of had motive. Maybe it's someone who doesn't need one. An undetected looney tunes."

"Lord, I hope not! It's what we're left with.

"Sergio, it wasn't some transient thing. If it was, Finch wouldn't be here to kill her. I'm convinced he did.

"What we have to find is what would serve as a reason for him to kill her. It wasn't any thrill killing. Not close to his type! He came here specifically to kill her."

"He came here purposely to kill her and to make it appear as though Vanderhaven had killed her. I've wondered about that. A lot! Why try to implicate Phil Vanderhaven? That's another point that doesn't make any sense!

"Motive is almost always love or money or rage or self-preservation. We don't seem to have any of that here, which leaves a nutcase."

"I can't quite accept that. Nutcases don't go to this degree of planning and setup. They're usually strong reaction killings for some slight or imagined slight that would ... I wonder!"

"I wonder about a lot of things. What?"

"How did Artie Finch get involved with these people in the first place? He doesn't fit, no matter what."

"That was an issue from the start for me. He doesn't fit. How when and why did he become involved?

"I think it's time to talk with Sherri. She might know."

Clint considered. "No. Let me talk with Eddie about this. I don't want to have to tell Sherri that she doesn't get everything yet. If I'm talking with Eddie, that won't come up. If it does, that will tell me something."

Sergio's turn to nod.

Pieces Begin to Fit

"Hi, Eddie! Sherri's not with you?" Clint greeted. He'd waited to approach Eddie until Sherri had gone into the Suites.

"She went to her room. She wants to rest awhile. It's been exhausting, but we had some fun. We didn't learn much of anything except it probably wasn't Vanderhaven the girls saw here in the bar."

"No. It was Artie Finch."

Eddie stared. "Finch? He was here? What does he ... he's not ... Finch?"

"Yes. Finch. He tried to make it look like Vanderhaven was here. We have to know he killed Tammy, but we can't find why.

"What can you tell me about him?"

"But ... Finch? He wasn't part of ... I mean, he was just there a few months ago. He was at ... I think maybe Phil was doing a sculpture of him. We all wondered why. He has the build for it and the looks, but he's crude. He was the type Phil would do before he got to where he had people who contracted for his work. He's the best you ever saw. You think the statue is going to turn around and say hello or something. He gets a lot of money for that.

"Maybe Sherri would know. I think she got drunk or stoned a time or two and ended up in his bed. She's more able to accept those types than most of us. I know Tammy told him she would rather fuck a pig than him.

"Sherri said his father is some kind of mob boss in Texas or something. I think she thought that was exciting."

"Yeah. Some women are attracted to what they consider

dangerous types.

"Do you have Vanderhaven's phone number? I'd like to talk with him."

"Yes. I'll write it down for you.

"I suppose Sherri will be relieved in a way. She was saying she was scared shitless that Phil killed Tammy. She was considering marrying him. He might have killed Tammy to get the extra money.

"I told her there was one thing that I knew for certain. It's that Phil couldn't care less about money. He could make an easy five million a year with his sculpture. He did that two years ago!"

They talked a bit more. Clint finally said he had to get to the station and home. He'd talk again later.

Clint called Vanderhaven and told him quite frankly that Finch had killed Tammy and was trying to make it look as if he did it. Where was he the past week?

"The past week? I'm in my studio in Napa doing a figure. A rock idol I won't name yet. She's been with me. It's finished and ready to ship. It's waiting for the truck.

"Where are you? You say Tammy has been murdered? I didn't know anything about it!"

"I'm in Bocas del Toro, Panamá."

"Where Sherri met that Indio she can't stop talking about? She even says she'd pay for a sculpture of him if she thought he'd agree."

"Guillermo? He would be the perfect study! He'd seduce you within five minutes."

"He's gay?"

"Bi. Like almost everyone here. He's with Tammy or whoever wants him. It's how he makes a living."

"Finch tried to make you think that I killed Tammy?"

"He tried to make people think he was you. It was a little overdone. I just wondered why he would try to implicate you, personally."

"I don't have anything to do for a few weeks. I'll come there. I think I want to meet this Guillermo. If he's half of what Sherri and you say he can seduce me. He already has and I'm never met him!

"I'm bi. I make no bones about it. I can come right away. As soon as I can book a flight."

"That might be a good idea. I can have you on a flight anytime you're ready. A friend has a major part of an airline."

"It's ... ten fifteen. I can be at the airport by two, packed and ready. Anytime after that."

"I'll have Pancho call you and tell you when the next flight leaves. It'll be to Panamá City. I can have a chopper there to bring you here if it's not a time when there's a flight."

"You have a chopper ready? You must have as much money as our little group!"

"I don't have much else to spend it on down here."

Clint soon called Pancho DeGulio. Pancho had recently visited him on the comarca. He said he'd have the regular two ten flight held if Phil couldn't get there in time. He would call Phil and make the arrangements.

It was just five in Bocas. Vanderhaven could come on the morning flight from Panamá City.

Some people were due for quite the surprise!

He called Manny and asked some questions. He got the answers he expected.

Tomorrow he might get the final answers. His serious suspects were now down to just three. Reactions would show whether or not the one he was sure was behind it really was.

He went to his house and took Nick and Janet to dinner at

Refugios. They had a fun night. They went back and to bed about midnight.

"He does look like the picture," Sergio noted. "He's a very handsome sort. You say he's bi, so Guillermo will like him if his personality is as you say.

"I don't know why you wanted him here or why it matters if he is bi."

"I think I know what's behind this. It's not money from the killer's perspective, but is from the perspective of the one who made the plan. It's shock time for a couple of people!"

They went to Vanderhaven as he came inside to introduce themselves. They had him booked at the Bahia.

They went out to the police truck they would use as a taxi. Guillermo was standing there talking with a pretty gringa who was there to catch her flight out. She looked tired and very satisfied. Clint grinned and asked if her stay in Bocas had been pleasant. She said she never knew it was possible for anything to be as pleasant as this one had been.

Sergio introduced Guillermo to Vanderhaven, who was obviously taken. Clint winked at Phil and said, "Guillermo, would you be willing to pose for a sculpture, nude?"

"Okay. Will it take long? I have to make a living."

"I'll pay for your time. Will a million dollars cover it?" Phil said, getting into the spirit of things.

"Twenty five dollars per day and we sleep together. It's my regular rate."

"Ah, yes. You are a whore, according to Sherri."

"The twenty five, yes. The sleeping because I think you'll be plenty fun. I've had nothing but women for two weeks and can use the change."

They got in the back of the truck to head for the Bahia

Hotel. They joked all the way. When Guillermo had Phil settled in his room they came back downstairs to head for Chitres for a delicious typical lunch.

While Guillermo and Phil were still upstairs Sergio asked what the hell this was about. Clint said it was to set a mood.

"A mood about sex? I don't get it!"

"I want the bisexual bit to be totally expected and natural. I need to know the reaction of one person."

"Baines? Sherri?"

"Not really. Finch."

"Finch?"

"Finch. Manny arranged for him to come back like it or not. I think he'll tell us what I almost know as fact."

"Who hired him?"

"He wasn't actually hired. He was tricked. It will make him go ballistic when he sees that."

"And he'll give us the one behind the whole sick scheme."

"Sick is a good description, I'd say."

Guillermo and Phil came back down. They had their lunch, then Guillermo said he and Phil would go to some places Guillermo knew about.

Clint had talked with Guillermo and told him to try to see that Sherri and Baines didn't know Phil was there. It was to be a surprise when they got together tonight at seven thirty. They would all meet at Ben and Earl's for a gourmet dinner. Phil and one other person were the big surprise. Guillermo asked if he was to not sleep with Phil. Clint said that was up to them. Phil was no part of the real problem. Just be totally as natural as he always was. If something happened with Phil, that was fine. If it didn't, it didn't.

Clint and Sergio went to the airport to meet Finch two hours later. He was surly and just short of threatening. He claimed he was as much as kidnaped and forced to come here.

"You were here a couple of days ago to kill Miss Sheridan," Sergio countered. "This is your chance to get some understanding of what was done to you and by whom. You will answer to justice for that, but there is no reason to make things any worse than they are.

"We can let you stay in the Sagitario at our expense or can hold you in a cell. Whichever, it is your choice. You'll find we're a lot more civilized than the bunch you were raised around.

"As stated, you were used and manipulated. I would tend to think you'd be most interested in knowing who did it and how it was done.

"Understand one other thing. You will get a sentence of perhaps six years here that will begin immediately or you can be sent back to the United States with all evidence. There you will face two or three years of courts and pleas, meanwhile being held in a cell. You will then face a sentence of twenty years. You will have been out and free for the last fifteen of those years should you prove to have the intelligence to see it.

"You will believe that your father can arrange something in the United States. Bear in mind that he couldn't even keep you there right now. Wonder who and what we have that nullifies what he has. Act accordingly."

Finch stared at Sergio a moment, then looked at Clint. "Is he for real? I can stay at a hotel when I have a murder, er, manslaughter charge against me if I promise not to cause trouble or run or whatever?"

"Yup! As real as they come!" Clint answered. "There's no lesser plea here. Manslaughter is murder. This wasn't particularly heinous so you're already facing a minimum charge.

If you argue, it gets worse. This is an island. There's nowhere to run.

"I think you'll give us what we need. I doubt you appreciate being put into a situation where only you could lose.

"I'll ask only one other thing. You don't go anywhere you might be seen by anyone who's connected with your little California clique."

"Gonna spring them on me to see who pisses in her pants?"

"Something like that. Do you like paella?"

"If it's made right!"

"By a master chef. Be ready to go to dinner tonight at about seven thirty."

"Cool."

"Nobody says that anymore."

"I do."

Sergio took him to book into the Sagitario. Clint went home to get things ready. Earl would make what was probably the best paella any of them (except Judi, Sergio, Guillermo and Clint) had ever tasted. They knew and were friends with Earl and Ben. They and umpty hundreds of others had already pronounced it the best.

Clint found Sherri and Eddie and said they had a big surprise dinner tonight. Be ready at seven!

They said they'd be there! They had never enjoyed a vacation as much as this.

"That's a terrible thing to say with my sister dead, but it's true. She would have wanted us to enjoy this place."

"A murder seems so ... out of place here," Eddie said. "I feel guilty for having fun."

"Well, we'll clear that up as fast as we reasonably can. We know who killed her. It's a matter of filling in a few details," Clint said.

"Vanderhaven, wasn't it?" Sherri asked.

"No. His alibi is as solid as a granite tombstone. He couldn't have possibly done it."

"He could have hired it, I suppose?"

"Anybody could arrange it to where they would seem safe.

"See you at seven! You know where Ben and Earl live?"

He told them how to get there and went to his house to get things ready.

Dinner and Dessert

Ben and Earl had a big table that seated twelve. Earl was a master chef by occupation. Ben also was a damned good cook.

Nick and Janet were seated on one side with Guillermo and Phil next to them. Finch and Earl were on the other side opposite Nick and Janet. Clint was at the foot of the table, Ben at the head. Eddie and Sherri would be seated in the center of that side. Sergio was on Clint's end.

Everyone was seated except Earl and Ben. Sherri and Eddie would be there in minutes. Ben poured some special wine and was about to give a welcoming speech when Sherri and Eddie came in.

Sherri let a small yelp escape when she saw the people seated at the table. Eddie looked very puzzled. He raised an eyebrow at Clint.

Ben poured them wine and went back for the welcoming speech.

"Welcome all! I'm Ben. I've been introduced to all of you except Miss Sheridan and Mr. Baines. Clint arranged this dinner party so he could do a Nero Wolfe or something as silly. We all know who killed Tammy." He nodded at Finch, who looked confused and a little nervous.

"Anyhow, it's a chance to show off for Earl and me.

"Oh! Sherri and Eddie, Earl is my lover. He's a master chef. You're going to eat the best paella any of you ever tasted tonight! He's even outdone himself!

"So! Dinner is served! Bon appetite!"

Earl rolled in an enormous tray with a huge platter of paella and plates. If it tasted a third as good as it smelled it was exceptional.

It was. Clint had to agree Earl had outdone himself.

When they had finished the dinner Clint stood and said dessert would be served shortly.

"I would like to ask a few questions if I might.

"For instance, how did Artie get introduced to your group?"

"His father wanted a sculpture of him. He said Artie was the only really handsome man in the family for years," Phil answered. "Seeing his body was like looking into a mirror, I had to agree.

"Excuse me if I'm vain. An artist has a right to be!"

He leaned against Guillermo, who laughed and hugged him.

"We're both shot right out of the saddle by Guillermo," he said.

"My god! Get a room!" Sherri snapped.

"We did. Where do you think we were all afternoon?" Guillermo fired back.

"How can you be ... I mean, you don't care if everyone knows?" Finch asked.

"Nobody cares, except they're all jealous of me for being the one with Guillermo," Phil replied.

"This isn't the states. If you've got an itch, what difference does it make which hand you scratch with?" Judi said.

"Is that what's behind you doing it?" Sergio asked. "You were pressured into it because you had slept with ... Phil?"

"And Tammy had said she would rather fuck a pig?" Clint added.

He didn't say anything for a few seconds, then said, "Because my father would have me hit if he knew. That's how he is. I would be an abomination against god and would disgrace the entire family."

"She blackmailed you into it? Why not just get rid of her?"

"She has pictures. Pops would get them."

"Er, Tammy had pictures of you? You killed her anyway!" Sherri cried.

"No. You had the pictures,"Sergio said. "You didn't know about the will she had made.

"Clint? Read her the important parts?"

Clint picked up the sheets by his plate.

"Due to some things I've learned, I am making this last will and testament before my lawyer, Mr. Miller.

"Should something happen to me, all assets of the estate I'm charged with administering will be divided as follows...

"There's a list of ten people who receive everything except the estate house. You already have two million, noted here."

"Will you verify that you were pressured and coerced into this by Miss Sherri Fordham Sheridan, Mr. Finch?"

"Oh, yeah!"

"Will you tell us about it?"

"Sherri and I had a little fling awhile back. A couple months or so. I was there because Phil was making a statue of me. He's damned good! I look like I'll smile and ask if you want a quickie any minute!

"Anyhow, Phil and I were together and I was naked and he made it plain he was interested in ... some things.

"I had never done anything like that, but he's handsome as hell and is a really good guy and it might be fun.

"I can tell you it was!

"There were a lot of pictures of me. Some of them had him in them. They were mostly for the statue and some for memory, you know? We were both naked and he was kissing me in one. One was really sort of, you know, a little too close.

"Sherri saw a couple like that on a table when she was there and stole them.

"See, I had tried to get Tammy into bed. She was kind of nasty about it and said I was a pig or something. She made me feel like a clod of shit! All I wanted was a little recreation for fun! I never said I loved her or any of that shit!

"Anyhow, Sherri said her sister had all the money and wouldn't even give her a little to buy a car she wanted, but she could get it all, and, after all, Tammy had cut me down to a stub that everybody knew about and made me a big joke to all her friends.

"I noticed that all her friends would stay away from me. It was pretty plain that she was mouthing off against me.

"Sherri made up some kind of plan about a contest that Tammy would win. She would get a free vacation. I said that was stupid. She could make her whole life a big vacation with what she had.

"Sherri said it would be a lark. It was the kind of thing her sister couldn't turn down. She'd been to all those places and knew Tammy would go apeshit in Bocas, what with people like Guillermo.

"I can see why Phil likes him. I think I could even maybe ....

"Anyhow. She said I looked just like Phil from a distance. Nobody here would know either of us. Tammy had refused to marry Phil so people would think he was pissed and had killed her.

"She wasn't the first I killed. Only the first woman.

"I thought it would be a way to get even for her making a joke out of me. I agreed. I did it. Here I am."

"So. It boils down to your father being a sadistic monster who would kill his own son for something as silly as having a romp with another man. Tammy rejected you. Her sister wanted her dead. You had killed before. You did it," Sergio said.

"Yeah. that's about it."

"I must now charge you with causing an unwarranted death. You will serve three years if you do not contest the charge."

"That would be stupid, seeing I admitted everything right here in front of a dozen people!"

"Okay. I'll arrange for your incarceration, Monday, so you have four days to prepare yourself. I'll not hold you if you'll remain here and cause no further problems."

"Thanks. I wish people in the states were half as human as you!"

"Miss Sheridan, I hereby charge you with premeditated murder. You will serve eight years should you not contest the charge."

"Are you out of your mind?! *I* didn't kill her! *He* did!"

"Under your plan and pressure, thus you are guilty of causing your sister's death through premeditation."

"I damned well will contest it! You can't prove anything!"

"We don't have to prove it. You have to disprove it. I do not see any possibility of that here.

"Mr. Finch will not run nor try to avoid his sentence, thus I will allow him his freedom until time to begin sentence. You are not of the same disposition and have stated clearly that you will contest the charges, thus you will be incarcerated until a hearing where the judge may suggest bail or incarceration.

"That can wait until after dessert! I saw Ben's famous cold key lime/ pineapple pie. I would not miss a chance at a small sample of that!"

They chatted, all except Sherri, who sat in a corner and refused to speak with anybody until she talked with her lawyer.

Sergio told her she could spend this one night at her hotel, but she would have to be jailed the next day. She left.

"She'll pay someone to get her out of Panamá by morning," Phil warned.

"Yes. I know."

"I don't get it! You can't let her get away with this!"

"She won't," Judi said. "Clint arranges these things so Panamá doesn't have to feed and house those type for years. She'll head for Costa Rica. Sergio will send all the testimony to California. It will show she as much as admitted it. She had solid witnesses against her who showed she planned and caused the death of her sister. She was in California at the time of the planning and the execution of the plan, ergo, she's now their headache. She doesn't have eighty million to spend on lawyers. She'll be convicted."

"She'll stay away from California is all."

"But she has no money unless she goes there to claim it."

"So. She has the option of facing it here, running to California where she'll be charged, or not being in either place. She'll end up a street person somewhere. She has no skills. Maybe a prostitute," Finch said. "Maybe she can go to Pops, who will have her hit because of what she claims about me. He wouldn't blink."

"I suppose they'll want your testimony in California. I'll allow you to go," Sergio said.

"No way! I'm convicted here and will have to stay! I can do three years standing on my head.

"Will they let me stay here after?"

"If you have been rehabilitated sufficiently and not declared undesirable."

"Well, I suppose I am, but so long as it's not declared...?"

"Clint can arrange it."

"Well, I have a sculpture to begin. I'll need to study the

subject very carefully before I can do it justice. I think I'll have to begin the research immediately!" Phil announced.

"Oh, bullshit! You already did some careful studies. You said so. This afternoon!" Judi pointed out.

"That was preliminary. I'll have to get into a much more intense mode for what will be the crowning achievement of my life and career!"

"Well, the crowning achievement of the year maybe. Let's go. I need some rest," Guillermo said.

"Ha! You're not going to get much," Sergio warned.

They went out, laughing and joking.

Nick and Janet said they'd heard Clint was like that, but Sergio had learned the lesson very well indeed!

Clint said he just wanted to get back to his wife and family. He had to get some rice and flour for her mother first.

A Short Visit

Clint and Tyna got out of his boat at his deck. Judi saw them and waved from her own deck. She called that she'd be right over.

Clint and Tyna would stay three or four days, then go to their place near Quebrada Tula for the next several months.

Judi came in and said it was good to see them. She and Tyna would fix a gallon of the fine coffee from a friend in the mountains. Coffee that good wasn't available anywhere. Chico grew and ground it himself. It was from a few plants by his cabin. He grew the commercial stuff, but this was a special plot of special coffee he shared with his closest friends.

Clint would go into Bocas Town to talk with people he knew. He would visit Sergio and Ben and Earl.

He went by the Golden Grill. In the past he would have stopped to chat with the regulars, but two had died and he didn't know the newer ones. He waved at the three he knew and went to the station.

Sergio was transferred to the main offices in Panamá City. He was head of education in police procedures, violent crimes. He was rated the top officer in the country in cases solved.

IIc hadn't wanted the job. He wanted to stay in Bocas, but he was the best. They needed him.

He claimed Clinton Faraday had taught him most of what he knew, that it was Clint who solved many of his cases.

Clint wasn't an officer. He was a special aide. He couldn't be conscripted into a teaching job.

Sergio had been in the position only a week when a case

came up that had the entire force stumped. He had done computer research that limited the suspects to six people. Solid alibis reduced that to four. Non-suspect witnesses eliminated two more.

He had two. He remembered when Clint had found a receipt in a bag in a garbage can, so went to evidence and through what they had.

Nothing – but there was a toothpick on a platter that had served sausages and olives.

DNA test time! DNA from either suspect would show they had been in a place they couldn't hope to explain.

Sergio personally arrested "Cuestick Carlos" for the murder. Carlos had been paid by the husband to kill the wife, who had a business and bank account in her name. He wanted to marry a woman he was having a long-term affair with.

"Clint Faraday taught me that the simple fact an object is too small for prints doesn't mean it holds no evidence. A DNA chain is one hell of a lot smaller than a toothpick or fingerprint!"

Naldo Vicente, the new head of violent crimes, grinned as Clint handed him back the report. "I was here for two months. Sergio taught me more in that time than I had learned in two years of university."

"Sergio is one hell of a good officer. Panamá needs more like him.I lost track of the last case here. I was going to follow it on the computer, but it slipped by."

"Oh, yes. Vanderhaven has moved here permanently. He made a pinkish marble statue of Guillermo that looks more alive than you could believe."

"Guillermo? He's still with Guillermo? That's hard to believe!"

"Oh, no. He's living with Osiria, that beautiful Indigeno

woman. Your wife's cousin, I believe. He and Guillermo are very close friends. I think Guillermo is the only man he's been that close to.

"The Sheridan woman managed to get ten percent of what cash she had in the bank in California by bribing a banker here – or in Ecuador. She's there now. They gave her amnesty when she bought a place. She can leave the hundred fifty thousand she has in the bank as a CD and live on the interest there if she's careful.

"Finch worked some odd deal where he's a personal attendant to a woman who owns some big almacen in Panamá City. He drives her around and sleeps with her. He gets to stay out of jail in house arrest. It helps that her brother is a bigshot politician! You know how that one works here.

"Did you know Manny's son is graduating from Panamá University next year with top honors? He's studied medicine and is going to be in charge of all those hospitals and clinics you, Manny and Judi built. "Sergio told me Manny was a crime lord in the states under a different name. I'm never to mention that to anyone but you and Judi and that strange Dave character.

"Dave was here last week. He's very spry for an eighty year old man. He's going to some place in the middle of the comarca in The Darien or somewhere. I'm thirty three and wouldn't do that!"

"It's what he does. We Indios take care of him even if he doesn't need it."

"He is popular with them. Every kid in the area calls him Abuelo Dave."

They chatted awhile, then Clint went back to his place. Judi was telling Tyna about the statue of Guillermo. There was a woman Clint didn't know sitting with them.

"... by the name of Rodgers said he's pay a million dollars for it, but Phil said it wasn't for sale. Some major arts magazine had a writer here to do an interview. She said she was in love with Guillermo from just looking at that sculpture. It was really fun when Guillermo walked in in person.

"You know Guillermo! He stripped and let her take pictures of him standing beside the statue. She took about fifty more than she could possibly need.

"Hi, Clint! I'm telling Tyna about Phil's marble statue of Guillermo. It's about the only thing anyone's talked about since he unveiled it last week.

"This is Leslee Albins. She was a friend of Phil and Eddie and the rest. She had to come here because of what she'd read about the sculpture. She likes the place, but more in the mountains. She's going to buy a vacation house above Volcan."

"It's beautiful there. It's quiet and cool. Judi was showing me the orchids around this place when I got here. My place has a lot of them. Dave, a friend of yours – oh, yes. He brought all these orchids – found one he said is very rare. It's beautiful! It's an Odontoglossum that he said is only found in Northern Peru. He found two others near my place last year. He said a lot of things that aren't found here are.

"It took a minute for that one to register.

"Cymbidiums should go riot there! I have a collection I can bring to plant. They do well in Northern California, but not too well in the southern end. They need cool nights the year-around.

"I'm excited. I never knew anything about Panamá other than the canal. It's heaven! The people are so nice, and they aren't impressed by Miss Rich Bitch Hoity-toit! I'm just another woman who might be a friend.

"I read about you back home. You're a very famous person in some circles. You're just 'My friend, Clint' here! I love it!

"Now that I'm running down, what are my chances with Guillermo? I have to meet him! Judi says she'll introduce us."

"If you've got the money, he's got the time," Clint replied. "He makes no bones about him being a gigolo."

"I saw that boy that he's supposed to be his father. He's only seven years old and is going to be a hunk! He'll be a gigolo by the time he's sixteen, I'll bet. I'll bet Guillermo was!"

"Try twelve or thirteen," Judi said. "He's honest about it."

"Yes. That's charming in its own way. I met that Sanders woman. She's a prostitute, but I'll bet he's like her. She says she's a nympho. Not many people can make the thing they like best their living!"

"There's no question of what Guillermo likes best," Tyna said with a laugh. "He's a sex addict in heaven!"

They talked and joked for a long time, then Judi took Leslee to meet Guillermo.

Clint sighed. He was as lucky as Guillermo. He had made what he liked best in life, the thing that would always have his interest, his main occupation.

It wasn't about money. Not that kind of thing. It was what he was born to do. He had more money than he knew what to do with. He still worked his ass off like any other Indio on the comarca. He was content. He had a place. None of those people from the states had a place. They spent their lives trying to find one. He'd found it after fifty years of searching!

He held Tyna close and brushed her hair with his lips. Twenty two years and he loved her more than ever.

He had it all! Eat your heart out!

A Vacation in Hell
© 2013 & 2020 by C. D. Moulton

Contents

A Vacation in Hell

Bon Voyage Party

Max Reede Took the small envelope from his PO box. A small bit of mail. Didn't look like an ad. From Kitti French? Who the hell was Kitti French?

Oh, yeah. Her. That dark fiery girl at Gene's party. The Halloween party. Goodlooking, and sexy as they come, but an attitude that turned him off within ten minutes of meeting her. Thought she was Queen of the May, or something. Whatever. One of Gene's weird friends. October 31, 2012, Celebrating the end of the world that was predicted to come in December – or something as goofy.

Gene would have weird friends. He was weird. Called himself a psychic student. Claimed he knew a true vampire, and was friends with several witches and warlocks.

Gene was from New Orleans. He spent a lot of time in Haiti and Jamaica. Eugene Lasalle. Mother was from Haiti, father was from Jamaica. Mother was part black and part French, father was French.

Gene had taken on a plan to convince Max that the voodoo crap was real. That would be a losing proposition, from the get-go! Max didn't have a superstitious bone in his body. All that stuff was was trickery, theatrics, suggestion, and hypnotics. Kitti's atitude started the minute Gene told her Max didn't believe there was any truth to the voodoo stuff.

That was ... he didn't pay a lot of attention, but she was supposed to be an apprentice of something or other. He'd said something like, "It's not my thing to try to scam anyone. I prefer honest work. Sleep better that way." She got all huffy about him saying she was a phony.

Hell! He hadn't! He'd said it wasn't anything he would be interested in. Nothing personal.

He tore open the envelope. Fancy penmanship! She should get a job where that would mean something in this age of e-mail and computer generated ads.

Mr. Reede -

I don't know if you will remember me. We met at a party. You said you didn't believe in certain rites as practiced in the Caribbean.

I own a place where I spend some time on Hell Island. I very much doubt you have heard of it.

Hell Island is a typical tropical Caribbean island. Palm trees and all that. Beautiful beaches, clean water, great fishing or snorkeling, surfing at some times of the year, very relaxed lifestyle. I always say the name of the place is like Greenland. The actual place is opposite what the name implies. The original settlers wished to do something to insure it would not be overrun with gaudy tourist traps and so forth.

I have a cabin on the water at Sunray Beach. It is a delightful place.

Make no mistake. There is much of what you call voodoo practiced there, but it is, as you will learn should you accept this offer, not an evil thing. It is more medicine and philosophy.

There are several there who do have a lot of power.

I propose that you take your vacation there. You have no one here, so Christmas in the Caribbean should appeal to you. Sun and palm trees instead of rain and frost. You will pay only for your food and so forth. You will only promise to care for the place as though it were your own. You will meet and know some very interesting people. Perhaps you will begin to understand us.

There is a place in the interior of the island where there are hundreds of tales of a great lurking evil. I think only that area is anyplace you would wish to avoid. While Hell Island is exactly one eighty from its name, El Diablo Mountain and the Valley of Lost Souls are truly descriptive. Should you challenge the old tales, it is on your own head.

I am aware that you took a dislike to me. I also reacted in that manner toward you. I very possibly was wrong, as were you, also. I make no claims of anything else. I feel you will wish to challenge the mountain and valley. I feel you will come back a different person, should you do so and survive.

There is the challenge, Mr. Reede! How will you answer it?

Should you accept this invitation, the party at Eugene's place Friday night can be your Bon Voyage party.

Will you be there? My crystal ball tells me you will.

Kitti French-

"A vacation on a Caribbean island, where all I pay for is food and, I imagine, transportation? You're on!"

"Well, Max! It seems you accept the challenge from Kitti! Welcome to your bon voyage party!" Gene greeted. "Come on in.

"Yo, everyone! The guest of honor has arrived! I'm too cheap for champagne, so bring out the beer!"

Kitti French came to grin at him. It wasn't what he expected, that it would be a sneering grin. It seemed more impish. They talked about the place. She said she was going there, by boat, Monday. He would be taken to the island when she went to get some things from the cabin, there. He could move right in.

"Monday?"

"Yes. Mama Bernadette said you would accept the challenge, and would be starting your vacation tomorrow, so would be ready. She's never wrong. She said to remember to bring your Glock, but you won't use it. It will make you feel more secure. Bring two tetracycline capsules. You will want them because of the change in water.

"I don't know what that means, but, as I said, she's never wrong. The rechargable batteries in your lantern will fail. They haven't been used much, so deteriorated. Because of this mention you will check them and bring new ones. You *will* want them. She says your life will be saved because you will bring snakeproof boots. There are snakes in the valley and on the mountain. You will encounter a bushmaster.

"That is all from her. She can't predict past that. You will come to points in your life where you must make a choice, and they will be choices you will meet, there. Your fate is determined at each one. Something on the mountain will be a major decision. If you don't meet and pass that point, you will never leave the mountain.

"I warn you about that. I don't wish to be the agent who brought you to your death. Please heed the warnings of Mama Bernadette. Me, I can be wrong. She is never wrong.

"I think you will survive, and will be a better person, one who has a greater understanding. I also think you will know emotions of an intensity you have never dreamed of."

"Yo! Kitti! Phone!" Gene called. She went to speak for a few minutes, then came back to say, "Mama Bernadette says to tell you to consider that a presence only she and two others have met will very possibility be there to meet you. She says to tell you it might be unwise for you to come. You will face a danger very few people have ever faced, directly. It will be a danger to your sanity. It will also be a direct danger to you in ways even she can't guess.

"Perhaps this was a bad idea, but she first said you would come. She said about the boots and ... I am confused. Mama Bernadette has never changed her mind, about anything. She says your very soul is in a period of flux. She can't predict. She doesn't ... I don't ... this was a bad idea! I meant to put you in a position where you would face truths, and would be taught a lesson, but ... I begin to fear this!"

Here goes the suggestion part, and the theatrics. Not gonna work, Honey! "Oh, I think I can handle it. We've gone this far, so I'll just go on. We'll see what happens."

She bit her lip, and shrugged. "Just so you understand that Mama Bernadette and I both think you shouldn't go. I'm completely serious. I didn't think it would come to anything like this!"

"I guess. What time Monday, and where?"

She told him the name of the boat, Sea Minor 7, and that it was in slip fourteen, at the marina. They would sail at six thirty. He wouldn't need a passport visa. There wasn't any government on Hell Island to check any such thing. He said he'd be there.

The party turned out to be fairly nice. He went home with Janice Linder.

He did have a few thoughts. Mama Bernadette did come up with a few things about him. A lot was logical progression. A few people carried tetracycline for when the change in diet and water left them with diarrhea. Kitti could have learned about most of it from friends, such as his Glock – but it was going to be a bit weird if his rechargable batteries actually were in bad shape. No one knew he even had the thing! It was true he hadn't used it in more than a year.

Don't start thinking about that kind of thing! The power of suggestion would be strengthened if he fell for the theatrics bit!

He'd get everything ready. He fully intended to have a good time on his vacation.

His rechargable batteries wouldn't hold a charge. He bought new ones.

Unwelcome to Hell Island

The boat trip to the island was beautiful, and really very pleasant. He expected Kitti would keep up the suggestions, but she didn't, beyond saying she thought he really shouldn't go into the interior, for any reason. He got to where he kind of liked her. She had a good sense of humor, which always appealed to him in a person. She was more than average intelligent. She was really a knockout in a bathing suit.

They made the wharf at the little town of Puddle. Kitti had no idea of where the name came from. It was three forty five on Tuesday afternoon. He went to the only store there to buy enough food for a few days. She said to buy kerosene for the refrigerator. There was no electricity on the island, except the small generator at the store in town. The town was seven buildings used for whatever, and a dozen or so houses. Nothing was open, but the owner of the store came when Kitti called her. She was introduced as Mrs. Freeling. She just grunted when Max was introduced. She was a heavy woman in her late forties or early fifties, with a bad disposition, it seemed.

Jon LeMond had the ATV used to deliver anything that needed delivering. He said, "Grmpth." when introduced. Liam Desmond had the place that sold kerosene. He didn't acknowledge the introduction. He said he sold kerosene Wednesday and Saturday, but would sell him some today, because he was with Kitti, and he knew she had to go places a lot of the time. Seven fifty a gallon, cash. No credit.

Mark Renault, the captain of the boat, spoke to Kitti for a minute, then went to the boat and brought a five gallon can of kerosene after they left Jon's. He wouldn't need that much, but seven fifty was far too much. It was six to six and a quarter almost anywhere on those islands. The food had seemed cheap to him, but Kitti said they charged him about half again what they charged the natives. She had warned him that they didn't want visitors there. They would treat him a lot better when they learned he wouldn't be staying long.

The cabin was really very comfortable. It was almost a kilometer from the nearest neighbor – who he doubted would speak to him if they were close. That was probably a good thing. He wouldn't annoy anyone, and they wouldn't annoy him.

They quickly went through the cabin. Kitti explained whatever needed explaining. She got a few things to take back to the boat with her. When she was ready to leave, she took him out back of the cabin to point through the trees to El Diablo. She said the valley was just before.

"Max, I've gotten to know you a bit. I think you're a good person. Please forego the mountain.

"Here's Mama Bernadette's number. Call her before you do anything. Please! Please follow her advice about things. She really does have the power. Have a good vacation, meditate, or whatever, catch up on your swimming and fishing and beachcombing – okay?"

"I'll see how I feel about things tomorrow. No promises today. I want to get the feel of the place. I'll talk to Mama Bernadette."

She bit her lip, and nodded. He wished her bon voyage, and she and Mark got on the ATV trailer and left. He went inside, put his things in the bedroom, fired up the refrigerator, and went swimming. When he came back, a woman and teenage boy were sitting on the porch. He greeted them, and said his name was Max.

"What you want here, Mon?" the woman asked. She didn't bother to introduce herself or the boy.

"I wanted to have a nice vacation and study some things, but that might not happen. Everyone here's so damned rude."

She looked thoughtful, and nodded. "You got the guts to say what you think. Won't nobody bother you, you don't bother them first and don't bring others. This here ain't no tourist mecca, and ain't never gonna be.

"What you study mean somebody else comes here?"

"No."

"Good! I'm Lucy and he's Sam. Ain't the sociable type, but you done figured that, less you stupid. Heard Jon and come to see what's what. I got a place in there (she pointed toward the right and inland). Ain't nobody else close. Bout a kilometer."

"In the valley?"

"You daft er what?" Sam demanded. "Ain't nobody in the valley! Nobody alive, nohow! Don't nobody even go close to there! You goonie er what?"

"He ain't from 'round here. He don't know nothin' bout the valley," Lucy said. "You gonna study in the valley?"

"I might. Maybe on the mountain, too!"

"Not just daft! Crazy as uh wankle bird!"

Max grinned at Sam. "You're not the first to say that!"

Sam laughed. "Probly not uh bad guy! Don't go in there. You never come back. Six people I knowed of went in. One come back and dropped dead three days later! Off his head, total! Only one alive who come back from thuh mountin uz Mama Bernadette, but she got the power. She go to thuh valley some 'n talks with the dead, but she say it ain't thuh dead. She say they ain't from here 'n ain't dead's all."

"What does that mean?"

"Damned'f I know!" Max laughed, and said he wasn't so bad, either.

Lucy said they had to get home before dark. They left. Sam grinned and winked.

Max went inside to fix some supper. He wondered what that was about. Sam was a naturally friendly person. Lucy was beyond what he could figure.

Was she afraid of him? Why? Was she just, as she said, antisocial?

He was definitely going to have to speak with Mama Bernadette.

He laid out everything he felt he would need, watched the magnificent sunset, then sacked out for the night. There were strange noises, and he was pretty sure someone came to look in the windows. He had the Glock on the nightstand, within easy reach. He wasn't going to let this bunch scare him.

Actually, he was amused by what he figured was a bit of theatrics Kitti had set up to get him into a suggestible mood. He didn't think there was actual malice, anymore. This was more a fun thing with her that would convince him she actually did have voodoo powers.

Maybe she knew the methods and tricks, but that didn't mean power. There was evidence that some people had a sort of psy power, maybe Mama Bernadette. Not Kitti.

He wondered what Mama Bernasette would be like. Would she be a craggy hag with an evil eye, and all that shit?

He'd find out. Tomorrow.

Mama Bernadette

Max got up to make a pot of coffee and have a glass of orange juice and a couple pancakes with guava jelly. He sat on the little porch facing the Caribbean to watch a sunrise that was easily as spectacular as the sunset had been last night.

He was very well-rested. There had been some noise during the night, but he didn't let it bother him. It was all what he expected on a tropical isle that was four fifths jungle. The cabin was more than comfortable.

The view from the little porch was toward the northeast. The cabin was back about eighty feet from the high tide line, and maybe sixty feet high on a low promontory. There were a few palm trees between him and the beach, which was a fairly wide band of pinkish sand. A pebble and small rock path led to the beach. There was a tiny island directly out, maybe a little more than half a mile, then open water to the horizon. Toward the left were some larger islands, but at a distance of more than ten miles, was his guess.

The tide was about half, he thought. The beach was fairly flat. Judging from when he first saw it at a lower level, the tide was probably only about two feet, at most. It was only a few days before the full moon, so the tides were at their highest level.

He took out his cell phone and was about to call Mama Bernadette, then thought about it.

Not smart! It was five minutes to six! He was always up early, but most people probably weren't! He'd wait until eight.

He went inside to heat the coffee and pour another cup, then went out the back to the little porch there. He could see El

Diablo, looking like a typical tropical mountain, with a few light clouds below the peak. The form showed him it was probably a dead volcano.

There was a strange hooting sound from above, He searched through the trees to see two monkeys sitting there, watching him. He waved, and called, "Good morning!" They chattered at him, and soon went away. He grinned. It seemed he did have close neighbors – of sorts!

He went to sit again, and glanced toward El Diablo.

What the hell! The sky was a lime green! The mountain was a dark shape. It was downright surreal!

He shook his head, and looked at his coffee. Had someone come during the night and put some kind of hallucinogen in it?

No. It was vacuum sealed. The seal hadn't been broken when he opened it to make the coffee.

He didn't see how they worked that, but supposed they could be using something he absorbed, or in the air, or something.

He looked back at the mountain. It was normal and serene.

He went back inside to wash the cup and put everything back in place. He went to the little bathroom to shave and so forth, then put on a bathing suit. He would beachcomb for awhile, then call Mama Bernadette when he got back.

He went out on the porch, then stopped.

There were no locks on the door! He hadn't noticed when they came, but they just opened the door and came in!

He shook his head, and turned toward the path.

"There are no locks here. We have no thieves or such. I'm Bernadette LeGrange," a rather pretty woman, about 35, medium complexion, light brown hair, slightly plump, said. "You could have called at six. I awaken by five.

"The green view was because you were noted by ... people. It probably will not happen again. If you ... yes. You have a good memory, if not photographic. I remember when it happened for me. It is actually quite beautiful.

"You wished to consult with me. Kitti was more impressed than she would let you know. She is greatly afraid that you are in grave danger here – which you are. I am seldom confused by what you would call my talent. With you, I am very much confused. There are a minimum of three equal paths you may take, each with branches. You are the second person I have ever met who has no fixed future.

"I'm afraid I can give little advice until you select a path.

"I have seen until the moment you enter the valley. The first branch of the path is there. I can see very little of what would happen on either path."

"You obviously know who I am. You're nothing like I expected."

"Yes. People would think I'm an old crone who cackles a lot, or a flambouyant voodoo queen from the movies. I'm actually a rather normal sport of person with a talent."

"You seem educated. Your English is better than mine."

"Loyola, ninety nine. Master's in social science, if there really is such a thing."

"I am surprised. That has a lot more effect on my ideas than the theatricals and tricks. As Kitti probably told you, I don't believe in any of that stuff."

"Kitti didn't say, but I knew that when she asked if she could send you here to learn a lesson about the realities of the arts. I have to say most of it is trickery or chemicals, with some hypnotism thrown in. It does often depend on suggestion. A few people have a psy talent. We're born with it. They can study it all they like, but it can't be taught or learned. It's there, or it's not.

"You want to know about the mountain and valley. I can only say that the talent is of little use there, except communication. I have almost no knowledge of what is there, but it is not evil. It just ... is."

"My personal theory. Evil is in the use of a thing. Things are not evil or good. They just, as you said, are. A knife is not evil, only its use."

"A true bit of philosophy. If a knife is used to cut vegetables, it is not because it is good. If it is used to kill, it is not because it is evil. There is a correalisation with the valley. Because very few ever return who go there, it is not the fault of the valley. It is because of something that is there. My talent didn't save me after finding what it is, it kept me from being where I would encounter it. It was like something in my mind said I was not to take this or that trail. I avoided those places, and found nothing much bad in the valley. I felt there was great danger, but it was not evil, so I have no idea what it might have been.

"Have you heard of the theories of planal distortion? The kind of thing that well may be what the Devil's Triangle is about?"

"Yes. There is something such here? Is that what you're saying?"

"Yes and no. It would explain much. I think it may have something to do with the valley. I believe taking a certain path will lead to a certain fate. I feel that is why I cannot fathom your future. You haven't yet been fated to any definite path.

"If you are determined to go, as I see you are, trust your, what you call 'gut reactions,' in a given situation. Carry your lantern, though it is early morning. Wear your boots. Those things will happen."

"In the valley?"

"And just before."

"What about the mountain? What is there?"

"El Diablo is a dormant volcano. There are things there that ... there are things there. You will meet them, if you survive to reach the mountain. Do not react with fear, and there will be no need of it.

"If you do, I can tell you from personal experience, do not go between the two arrowhead-shaped white rocks. Go to either side, and you will be in a place where you would not be if you go between them. You will just be on the mountain.

"I had a premonition, the first time I went there. I held the end of a string, so found my way back. Had I not done that, I would very likely have never returned here.

"I have no real knowledge of what I encountered there. I have what seem to be memories of meeting El Diablo, in person. That is the gate to hell. Other, I know exactly. It is for your exploration, not my saying.

"I have a personal theory that one passes into another reality when she goes between those rocks. That I met and spoke with El Diablo is most doubtful, but I did meet and speak with a strange being not of this world. I will not suggest what you may find if you go there. I am not certain I believe what I found will not impres you as truth.

"I studied Latin and Classical Greek at Loyola. I have to admit those languages proved very useful. I know you studied some Greek ... that your great grandmother was from Greece, that you learned to read the language to be able to read and understand the classical mythology. If you can put the proper sounds to the words, perhaps you will be able to commun- icate.

"There isn't much more I can tell you. I know my advice to forego a trip into the valley, thence to the mountain, should you survive, would be rejected.

"I will go back to Puddle, you will go to the valley.

"Take food for two days, minimum. There is plenty to be found in the valley, but – this part I don't know – it isn't all safe to eat. I know when a thing is not good. You have no such talent."

She changed the subject. They talked about the states and people she knew, then she headed back toward Puddle.

He got the things he would need to start on his little excursion.

He wasn't quite so flippant, after talking with Bernadette.

<u>Valley of Lost Souls</u>

The first kilometer was fairly easy going, but the path ran out just before he reached the pass into the valley. It was obvious that no one had gone through there in quite a long time. The brush was impenetrable. He had to use a machette to cut a way in.

It took almost two hours to go through the pass, only about a kilometer. When he broke out the other side, the going was much easier. He stopped to look down on the lush valley with a small silver river winding along the bottom. El Diablo was magnificent, from that spot. It was a breathtaking vista.

He started to move forward when something hit his boot, only half an inch from the top. He saw a brownish snake with black X'es on the back. A bushmaster! Had he been wearing regular shoes, it would have bitten him! He was miles and hours away from any possible treatment. He would never have left the Valley of Lost Souls!

He decided not to chase it. It was a thing of the place. It was unlikely anyone else would come through to be threatened by it. He would certainly proceed with a lot more caution!

Fifteen minutes later, he came to a branch in the slight animal path he was taking. He saw they both went on downward, but one branch went more to the left, not so directly toward the mountain.

He almost started along the more direct path, but felt uneasy. He went back and down the other. He felt nothing unusual, there.

There was a mournful cry to his right. It sounded like ... nothing he had ever heard. A banshee? It sent a chill though him, and he felt the hair stand up on the back of his neck.

Did that other path lead to whatever made that cry?

He didn't really want to know. He did wonder if Mama Bernadette could read more of his future now.

What? He was getting brainwashed ... but she was right about the lantern batteries and the boots. He was glad he brought food and the lantern ... and his Glock. He had quite a lot of lightweight equipment in his special backpack.

He went on for an hour and a half, and came to the river. The water was clear and clean. There were tropical fishes of various types. He saw a school of yellowish-brown fish with bright scarlet throats.

Pirahnas? Here? Weren't they more an Amazon fish?

The water there was fairly deep. He wasn't about to go into it!

He could go either way along the river. It seemed more likely he would find a place to cross upstream, so he turned that way.

Another branch in the path. Would he have felt anything if he'd gone left instead of right?

He turned around, and started moving. He immediately felt something like ... he was being watched?

He looked down into the river. The pirahnas were there, moving along with him.

He turned back. The fish stopped. He started the other way. They didn't follow.

If he went down the river, would he come to whatever made that cry? Would he be forced to face it or the pirahnas?

Do *not* let your imagination get started here! He went on for twenty minutes or so and came to a rocky set of rapids. He could, with some difficulty, cross there.

He thought. He sat on a rock to eat one of his sandwiches and drink a can of peach nectar. He took the can and wrapper to drop into a plastic bag, which he hung on a strap to his backpack. He did not toss garbage on the ground. Ever.

He decided to go a bit more upriver to see if there was a better place to cross. He didn't think the pirahnas would come up the rapids, so the more between him and the unobstructed river, the better.

That was a good idea! He came to a swinging bridge across between two rises by the riverside!

A bridge? Where no one ever came? It didn't make sense – unless people did come. They were trying to stop him from coming, so the tales about the valley were just that. Tales.

Mama Bernadette. He took out his cellular, and saw there was a signal, if not too strong.

He called her. When she answered, he told her about what had happened, to that point. He asked about the bridge.

"Bridge? There is no bridge that I know about."

He described it.

"I can't see anything about you. I know you have taken two paths, both the safe ones. I don't know if the bridge is another choice you have to make. I didn't know of its existence.

"Max, I like you. I sense there is some kind of approval of you by someone or something indistinct. It has to do with you and ... not ... dirtying something?"

"Not ... maybe because I ate a sandwich and drank a canned drink, and didn't leave the garbage?"

"Perhaps. I can't advise you about the bridge."

"Would you cross it?"

There was a silence, then, "No."

"Then I won't. I'll call later, if there's a signal."

He went back up the river a short way until he found a place he could cross without too much trouble. He went slowly and very carefully across, then found a path toward the bridge, and another toward the mountain.

He didn't hesitate. He went toward the mountain.

It was fairly easy going. He was almost halfway between the river and mountain when it started getting dark. He was surprised, but his watch said it was nearly seven. He'd completely lost track of time!

He had the light plastic tent with an air matress bedroll sewn in under it. He set up the tent and inflated the bedroll with the little attached pump, then made a rocky pit for a fire. He soon had the fire going, so put on some water for coffee and brought out some paper and pencils to write about what he had seen. He had taken a lot of pictures, at first, not so many, later. The camera had a four gig card. He could take a few thousands, if he wanted. He had plenty of recharged batteries for the camera.

He opened a can of tuna and fried it, then cracked an egg over that. He put it between two slices of bread, and had a good sandwich.

He hadn't realized how tired he was. He went inside the tent and to sleep. It was a lot earlier than he was used to, but he would be up early. He wanted to be at the mountain before midday, if possible.

About three in the morning he was awakened by noises outside. He sat up, and turned on his lantern. He opened the flap, to find himself face.to-face with a large monkey or ape! He turned the lantern into the face, and it raced into the trees.

Pirahnas, now apes? Here? There were no apes on any Caribbean islands!

Was it an ape? It was a lot *like* an ape, but the features were ... different. It didn't seem to run hunched over like an ape.

He was very damned glad he had his Clock! He sure as Hell wasn't going to get more sleep tonight!

He was also glad Mama Bernadette said he wouldn't have to use the pistol. What if there were a colony of apes there, that he shot one – and the rest tore him to bloody little pieces?

Was the cry he'd heard from one of those apes? Were they why no one ever lived who came there? Were those stories true? Was he a total idiot to be here, against all advice?

He was down in the valley a distance. The sunrise was about twenty minutes later than on the beach. He saw it was six fifteen, and called Bernadette. There wasn't a signal there.

When it was light enough, he went outside, Glock in hand and ready, but there was nothing there, and no sign there had been anything.

Was it a nightmare? Was the suggestion getting through? How had any such idea been planted? *Had* it been planted?

No. There had been no suggestion of anything like that.

He brewed some coffee and had two eggs on toast, packed his backpack, and headed on toward the mountain. His mind was telling him to turn around and get the Hell out of there!

That wouldn't be him. He had come this far. He would finish the trip.

He came to the mountain, two hours later. It was on a slow rise, then suddenly was more steep. There was a path to the right, and one to the left.

What was with all these animal paths? There wasn't much to indicate there were any animals using them. They were just ... there. Were they made by the apes?

He checked his phone. There was a fair signal. He called Bernadette. He got her, but there was a lot of static. He explained about his night, and the apes.

"They are not apes. There are no apes here."

"What are they?"

"That's the sixty four thousand dollar question. I never

directly encountered any of them, but saw some evidence, and, one time, caught a glimpse of something. It seemed a very hairy and very large person. Only a glimpse, then it was gone. I sensed curiosity, not a threat. There may only be the one. There may be several. I don't know. I get no feeling about them. It."

"Well, I'm at the mountain. Should I go right or left?"

There was a silence. "I don't know."

They chatted for a minute, then the signal faded. Max put the phone back in the pocket sewn into the backpack and looked up and down the path. He shrugged, and went to the right. He came to a cave that the path led into. He shone his lantern into it, but didn't see anything but a lot of loose rock. There were rats in the cave. Maybe they made the path. He turned around, and went the opposite direction. More than an hour later, he came to two arrowhead-shaped white rocks.

El Diablo Mountain

Max took a lot of pictures. He took this spot from several angles. He remembered what Mama Bernadette said, so went to the left of the rocks to take pictures that looked exactly like the ones from just before. He went around to the other side to take more. No difference.

He went back to stand in front of the rocks. He remembered what Mama Bernadette said, so took out a long roll of nylon twine. It was on a reel spindle that he attached to a strong limb. He tied the end to his belt, took a deep breath, and stepped into the space between the rocks.

There was a blurry few seconds, then the light seemed to be far more toward the green. It was a little lighter than the lime green he saw in the flash, and was quite beautiful. The plants seemed of different types than were in the area.

He turned to look back the way he had come. The nylon line seemed to just begin a foot or so above the path, which went on out across a flatter area. No valley, no river.

He stepped back to where he found himself between the rocks, staring out across the valley.

This was weird! That planal distortion theory had to be right!

He turned around, and went back into the ... portal? There was three quarters of a mile on the reel. He was going to do a bit of exploring!

First things first. He needed to know where this spot was from this side. There were no arrowhead rocks here.

He noticed the path had a break where the line appeared. it was like a line of turquoise across the path. There seemed to be a slight fog on the path, right there.

He went around the path to the side. He could go on that way. He came back along the path, and was past the line. Apparently, you went through the portal in only one direction. He remembered he had gone all the way around the rocks, finding no difference in the local landscape.

He went back to the path. He took two white pieces of cloth to tie to twigs on either side of the turquoise line. He stepped back behind the line to note they could be seen from either side of it. He then moved a couple hundred feet along the path, to see they were visible from a distance.

What now? Say he'd been to El Diablo Mountain, found an answer that led to dozens of puzzles, and go home?

Yeah! Like he'd ever had that much sense! He was here, and he was going to look for some answers.

He decided the best way to approach this was to move along that path. It was a lot more than the animal paths he had followed on the ... other side? This was mostly laid out with smaller pebbles poured in a line onto the sandy soil.

The plants were strange. Some were beautiful, some were odd, to the point of being scary. Flowers sometimes looked like bugs. He would use up the whole card if he took pictures at the rate he was going! He noticed there were a lot of thorny plants. He saw some bugs that were like nothing he'd ever imagined. The soil was a rich black, in this area, and his concentration was on random sweep, jumping from subject to subject.

There were a couple of little faint trails leading off to the sides. They didn't appear much used. They were probably animal paths, such as he followed on the other side. They looked like that.

He came to a rock wall. It was about eight feet high, with a wooden door across the path. A strange symbol was painted on the center panel.

Does that mean do not enter ... or do not exit? Is it advertising toothpaste, or something? Is it a for sale sign?

He took some pictures.

Decision time! Open that door, or turn back?

The smartest thing would be to see what he could before taking stupid chances

Maybe just open it and look?

What if there was an alarm attached ... or something?

He turned around. Why tempt fate?

He moved back a few feet when a figure stepped from one of the faint sidepaths. Its back was toward him, but he froze where he stood. He reached to take the Glock into his hand, then quickly pushed it back into its pocket on the backpack. Meeting a strange being with a weapon in your hand was a Hell of a long way from intelligent.

The being was moving away, but suddenly stopped, and spun to face him. It was a dark brown hairy being, very muscular, human-shaped. The fingernails and toenails were conical, just short of being claws. The face was as hairy as the body. The eyes were almost glowing, and were red. The mouth had two longer upper teeth among many sharp ones, almost fangs. This was a male – if not having teats meant anything here. All it was wearing was a sort of brief loincloth.

Okay. A male in Hell was a demon. This one looked the part!

The being made a short sort of growl, and moved toward Max. Max wished he'd kept the Glock in his hand. He was as much as paralyzed from movement.

Why didn't he feel threatened? If there was ever a time in his life he should have felt sheer terror, this was it! Yet, he didn't feel he was in any particular danger.

The demon stopped about two yards from him. It seemed curious. It spoke in a language that really did, as Bernadette suggested, sound like Greek. He spoke a very little from when he spent two weeks in Athens, six years ago. He knew the classical Greek to read, and had noticed the vowel shifts and such in the language.

Nothing to lose. Try to remember the correct words and the correct structure of the sentence.

"Greetings! I am called Max. What are you called?"

The demon cocked his head to the side, and what could have been a grin crossed his face. "Octon. You ? a very strange ? You have crossed into ? by ? ? ?"

"I have too few words. I came across the portal."

The demon laughed. Why? What had he said?

"? you to encounter ? when ??. I do not ? while ??. I will then introduce ? and ? to ?? you. Come."

Max decided he liked this demon. He was more trying to help than threatening. Hell! *(Stop thinking with that word, here. It's where you are!)* He wasn't in the least threatening!

Max moved to beside the big demon, who spoke very little. He did say that the person(s) he would introduce could communicate much better.

Problem! His line was running out! He asked about that.

"You do not ? it. You can return here ? ?. We will ? to ??." He took the line to tie to a bright purple shrub. There were very few of those in the area, so he could locate it easily when (if) he came back.

They went on for more than a kilometer. The path was, it seemed, the only one that was paved with pebbles in the area.

They went into a small pleasant valley, and to a stone cabin. Octon waved him inside.

Octon was a demon who looked only a little like Max felt a

demon would look. This one was a truly terrifying sight! He was a bit taller and more massively muscled than Octon, was deep black that set off the red eyes. He had longer fangs. He wasn't wearing the loincloth. There was certainly no doubt this was a male!

"This is Max, a ? ? came across the ?" Octon introduced. "Max, this is ? Arctus Julio.

"I will ?? to your ?" He waved, and left.

"Ah! Welcome to Hades, Max! Call me Juli," Juli said, in excellent English.

Max couldn't stop a short giggle. Juli asked why.

What the ... heck Be honest! "Juli somehow doesn't fit you."

Juli laughed. "Ah, yes! It is a woman's name, in your place! I am definitely not a woman!

"Have a seat. We can talk, then we can decide what to do with you. I think you'd be a bit tough, so dinner would probably not be a good idea."

<u>*Chat With a Demon*</u>

Juli looked serious when he said that. Max didn't know how to react, so nodded, and said, "I agree. Not a good idea." He tried to look as serious as Juli.

Juli laughed. "You have a very good sense of humor in a situation that actually is very dangerous to you. You didn't threaten Octon, or anyone, or you would be dinner, but for the bugs and bacteria, not us. Probably. I can't speak for others.

"I don't understand why you, Kitti, and Bernadette didn't react to us in the way our races have historically acted. You are much like Bernadette, in thought. She was curious, and likes to make jokes. Kitti found us to be ... attractive, but frightening. You seem to be between those two.

"Bernadette taught me the English. We spend about fifty times the time people think together. We have developed a deep affection. We have a place we meet in the valley in a part where it is safe for both of us.

"You seem to desire honesty. I will say, directly and truly, that there have been forty two of your people who came here, and only Bernadette and Kitti have returned. There are several who came into the valley who did not return. The two or three who did return died within days. That is not from us. We have lost two of our people in that valley. We almost never go there. Bernadette and Kitti have a special path they use through the valley. I think they told you of it."

"No. Bernadette said I would come to forks in the path. It was to me to discover the correct one. I have a slight bit of her talent, I guess. I would get a definite feeling about which path to take. There were three that I somehow knew would be the bad choice. I could see why on one, particularly. Crossing the river. There were pirahnas in it. If I'd taken the other way, it would put me between the pirahnas and something pretty terrible. There is a bridge across the river. Bernadette said she would not take it – I was speaking with her on my cell phone – so I didn't take it."

"A bridge? Why would there be a bridge where no one ever goes? Bernadette and Kitti both sense there is something terrible there, but they feel it may not leave certain areas. The trick, as Kitti says, is to know which places to avoid.

"You do not wish to know why none of the others survived to return to your place?"

"I can assume they either threatened you with a weapon or attacked you in another way, or died of heart failure. You are, after all, demons from Hell, in our legends!

"I considered showing a weapon when I first saw Octon. I felt that would be immensely stupid. It was a feeling like at the forks in the path. I was as much as paralyzed, but Octon merely seemed curious about me, and has a fun sense of humor. I immediately liked him.

"When I first saw you, my bones turned to jelly! Octon is a lot *like* the legends. You *are* the legend!"

Juli laughed. "Bernadette taught me a little joke. She said that I naturally would look like a demon from Hell. After all, I *are* one!"

Max laughed. He found he really did like these demons! They had great senses of humor.

"You have seen what happens when your people come here. Luckily, that is quite seldom. Long ago, one of our people, Dionysus, was killed, when two came through. He went to see what they were. He would have welcomed them here. We are a friendly and curious people. Since that time, we will defend ourselves, if attacked. We make no excuses.

"Bernadette has explained that the time and descriptions of the Dionysus encounter tells her a couple of pirates stumbled upon the portal. They were probably terrified, were deeply religious, they saw demons coming for their souls. They were wearing armor, and had weapons.

"Whatever, we make no apologies for defending ourselves. We are friendly people, who are also capable of extreme violence."

"I think the problem started centuries ago. You speak what sounds very much like classical Greek. You are in the legends from that time, and before. There is some evidence that a few of us had a great deal more psy power back then than now. They discovered how to open a portal, and used your people to gain and hold power over others."

"It would agree much with our legends. The portals were opened. Something made three of them remain. Two are very large, and are fluctuating kinds of things. They are to other realities, not this one. Bernadette says one is called the Devil's Triangle, and is close to the place she was born. There are tales of mighty ships and areoplanes disappearing into those. She thinks there is a different time in those, that it is different from here.

"You have a lot of science. We have little. You are not a generally happy people, we are. Perhaps there is a connection, perhaps not. Bernadette says there is a different psychology. Kitti says you are a decadent society, based on greed. I know little of such things. Both she and Kitti say the real problem in your reality is that the race breeds like insects and rodents, with no consideration of the obvious facts that all of your race's problems are due to overpopulation.

"Perhaps that is because you have no cyclic fertile periods, as in our race. We have much the same reaction to sexual situations, but we avoid such relations when they will lead to such problems. You do not."

"We have fertile periods. We merely choose to not control anything. Most women, particularly among those who, logically, should not breed, want a lot of children.

"We know what the problem is. We refuse to do anything about it. We have contraceptives and painless sterilization methods, but generally ignore them.

"What a strange conversation!"

"Yes! Isn't it?"

Max couldn't help it! He liked these people, the two he'd met!

"Well, we will have some food, and will talk. You may wish to stay here the night, or go.

"I almost forgot! It would not be intentional. You cannot eat the food here. It will poison you."

"I have enough for two more meals. Dinner tonight, and breakfast tomorrow. That is no problem. I can spend the rest of today and awhile in the morning getting to know you. I think I very much like you demons from Hell!"

They stayed together. Juli introduced four others, two females. While they did not appeal to him, he could see how those into bondage and female dominance would find them as much as completely irresistible!

Max liked every one he met. They were open and curious. They found him odd and fun. They made jokes about him being the demon, not them! It was all good-natured, not in any way hurtful.

He rested very well. He got some great pictures of the sunset and sunrise. Juli said the pictures wouldn't develop. He showed them the digital camera, and the pictures on the card. They noted the beauty of the sunrise and sunset, but the rest from there were ordinary. They were fascinated by the ones from his reality. The colors and forms were so different, mostly in subtle ways. The sunrise and sunset were such unusual colors!

About mid-morning, he headed back to the portal. Juli and Octon walked with him. They stepped out between the arrowhead rocks. This was the first time Octon had been outside his reality. He was fascinated, but nervous.

It seemed natural for him to hug these terrible monsters goodbye.

Crazy Man's Cave

Max didn't waste much time on his way back. He came to the cabin, to find Bernadette and Kitti sitting on the porch, waiting for him. Kitti said Bernadette saw that he was welcomed by the people on the mountain.

"They aren't on a mountain, in their reality," he pointed out. "Just among some hills. The mountains were in the distance, there."

Bernadette wanted to know all about it, so he explained everything. She said it was all as she knew it to be, but there was no bridge that she remembered. There simply would be no point in having a bridge anywhere in a valley where no more than ten people went in ten years.

She had followed a different path to the mountain. She came on the river quite a distance upstream. It was where two creeks ran together to form the river. There were easy places to cross both creeks. There was no bad path up there.

"Whatever is wrong in that valley is more to this part," he suggested. "There's something there. Whatever it is is restricted as to where it can go. We took paths outside of its territory."

"That's a lot like what I felt," Bernadette replied. "Perhaps that bridge is at the limit of its area."

"I think I want to go back and cross that bridge. I'm damned well going to have the Glock in my hand, and it's going to have the safety off!"

"I don't sense any reason not to cross the bridge. It's there for another reason," Bernadette suggested. "I don't think you will need the gun, but you will ... there is something ... insane? There is something or someone insane there?

"Take the greatest care. I sense there is ... are ...two things there. The one makes you safe, but only because the other is there. It isn't clear. I can only express it as the insanity is no danger to you because the ... alienity? Is there."

"Then the insanity would be from this reality, the other not?" Kitti asked.

"That expresses it well."

Max thought, then nodded. "Tomorrow, for the bridge. Today, to lay around and download all my pictures. I wonder if the camera can capture the shades and tones there. I hope so."

"I sense that the pictures are proof only to you, that others will claim you have merely altered the colors."

"It's a good thing I'm the only one who cares about proof, and it'll be fine if it's only to me. You two will know it's real."

"Different realities are what it's about," Kitti said, with a grin. He returned the grin.

Mama Bernadette said she would go back to Puddle. Kitti would stay. They could get to know each other. They would be friends, if not a lot more – but not to a level they couldn't both be comfortable. They would never love each other in any deeper emotional sense.

"More or less like you and Juli?"

"No. Juli and I take it to a far deeper place."

"But the Hadeans are great lovers!" Kitti said.

They joked a few more minutes, then Bernadette left, walking along the beach. Kitti went inside to cook a delicious meal. Max went swimming for awhile, had the meal, then cranked up his laptop to download the pictures. He used it for as little time as possible. He wanted to save the battery. He chatted and joked with Kitti. They strolled along the beach around the end of the island and back. That took three hours. They had a light meal, showered and such, then hit the sack – as Max hoped, by that time, together.

It was a great night!

In the morning, Max packed his backpack, made a few sandwiches, took some boxes of juices, and headed for the valley and the bridge. It was fairly fast going. He had followed that path both ways, so knew it. In a little less than two hours, he was standing by the bridge.

He suddenly felt danger behind him. He didn't hesitate to run across the bridge.

When he looked back, he didn't see anything ... or did he? He didn't remember passing that twisted driftwood tangle by the path! There wasn't any driftwood on the side of the mountain!

The "driftwood" moved to the end of the bridge. It didn't try to cross, though Max doubted it could. It was too big.

He took a series of pictures of the thing, part on zoom. The thing seemed to be looking for a way across the river. It raised itselt to about ten feet high, and made the horrible cry he had heard, it seemed, eons ago.

He turned to hurry along the path. He couldn't go back the way he came. He had to know where he could run if that thing crossed the river! Would it wait there?

Go on to the left. It wasn't back that way.

He was moving along a sort of cliff face when he came to a cave There was a small fire in a rocky bowl, with an old iron skillet on it. There was some kind of animal leg being fried in the skillet.

"It can't cross the river, young'un," a voice close to his back said. He spun, to see a skinny old man with grey hair to below his shoulderblades, holding a machette that was worn down to almost a thin sword.

"That's good to know! What in *Hell* is that thing?"

"Ha! That's a good one! What in *Hell* ... where we're at.

"I'm Carey. It's the devil, I think. Tryin' to get my soul fer more than fifty years now. Can't. Can't leave where God lets him roam. River here to thuh river over south to the mountain 'til the cliff up 'bout mebbe a thousand feet high. Can't go quite to thuh pits down there. Don't go under mebbe three hunderd feet high. People down there know to never go over that high. Don't never come, nohow. Only the ones the devil sends after me, but I know it's them. When they can't get me, he takes 'em. One done got away, and run back inta thuh town. Mind stayed up here. Body went back. Probly didn't live more'n a day er two.

"If'n I didn't see you wasn't from the devil, you woulda ended up the devil's supper, er what was left of ya. Done been nine of 'em ended up thet way!"

Was that why no one who came into the valley left? This madman cut them up with the machette?

"I didn't know anything about this place, three days ago. I heard some tales, but didn't credit them. They say the devil's on the mountain."

"He's here in the valley. Ain't nothin' on the mountain but some kind of ape people. Don't bother me, I don't bother them. Don't much care to go on the mountain. Ain't nothin' there most but mountain."

"Why do you stay here?"

"Uhcause God wants me to keep the devil from goin' out. Uhsides, got a curse on me God's protectin' me from. Got food'n water. Comfterble. Health ain't bad. Better'n most my age. I'm eighty six. Or seven. Fergit exact. See good, hear good. Got it easy!

"I was captin on a ship. Hurricane, I ended here. Nobody liked me, so I came here. God talked tuh me some. I got a agreement. I keep thuh devil in there an' got a easy life. Been here nigh on fifty years. Fifty one. Don't remember exact.

"See, I'm strong. Most what meets the devil is madmen 'n go crazy. I meets him 'n resists what he does, so God knows he can have me an not worry about the devil here. I didn't go looney from seein' him up close, like everbody else. I'm strong! Devil knows he got more trouble then he can handle if'n he gets off his, what I call 'reservation.' Like the Indians, 'n thet, y'know.

"See, I knows these here islands. I was borned on Barbados. Grew up with the devil worship people. Voodoo and magic stuff. They tried to git me dead, but all I got was thet curse. God done stopped that!"

"I see. What happens if they get rid of the devil here?"

"'N he goes somewhere they ain't nobody to control 'im? Anybody thet stupid?

"I guess they is. Sad what people will do."

"Yes. It's really sad to see what the world's become."

"Nother thing! I ain't got to look et thet!"

"Maybe you're the lucky one! I really don't much care for the idea of going back to that. I could stay on this island, I think. It would be okay if you can keep the devil from getting out."

"Done it fer fifty years. Fifty one. Don't remember exact. Fifty more, you got to get somebody else. I'll be past it, by then."

"Probably come to that. Nice talking to you, but I'd better get on back. I don't think I'll ever come this way again, but you never know!"

"Yeah, young feller. Good to have somebody to talk to, now and then. Wind ta yer back!" He went into the cave.

Well, that explained part of the reason no one went back from the valley. That weird tangle of driftwood or whatever answered the rest of it.

If you considered the other reality people as not being a puzzle.

They weren't a puzzle he needed to solve, more than he had.

Now! How to get rid of the devil here!

Did he really want to?

Priorities

Max came back to the cabin to find Bernadette and Kitti sitting on the porch, waiting for him.

"Did you find why the bridge was there?" Bernadette asked.

"Yes. I've learned some things. I saw what causes the problems in the valley. I have pictures." He took out the camera to show them the shots of the "Driftwood Devil," as he labeled it. They saw the first several, and shrugged. "What?"

He showed the thing where it was at the end of the bridge. Six shots as it rared up.

"Carey says it can't cross the bridge. He's has an agreement with God to keep the devil inside its territory."

"Carey? I'm afraid there's something in that area that prevents me from sensing anything. That's why I didn't know about the bridge – and, apparently, about people being there!"

"Just Carey. Part of why people don't come back is the devil, part is Carey, who thinks they're people the devil sent to take his soul. He knew I wasn't that, because the devil was chasing me." He told about his experiences. They were surprised Carey was there, and more because he was there for fifty years.

"Do you think we can get rid of that thing?" Kitti asked.

"I don't know. It's not a priority.

"I've been thinking about this situation. Can you tell me where the limits of danger are? I, rather obviously, went into the area of that thing on my first trip through. I told you my route. You seemed to have said you went to the west of where I went, so managed to avoid the places that thing can go. I sensed danger only when the thing was close.

"Can we get a fairly accurate layout, using your talent?

"I know, from Carey, it doesn't go below three hundred feet elevation, and can't go past the rivers east and west, or more than a thousand feet elevation. I want to know the outer design of that area. The perimeters."

Bernadette looked thoughtful. "Do you have paper ... no! You have a computer! Is is WiFi?"

"Yes. I've still got a lot of battery. About an hour and a half." He went inside, to bring the laptop to her. She went to MapQuest, then to another mapping program. She brought up an arial shot of the island, then zoomed in to the area she wanted. She quickly sketched the area, complete with the mountains and rivers.

"So! Did you expect that?" It showed the area Carey described was a very clear triangle.

"To tell the truth, yes.

"Bernadette, the other reality isn't in that triangle. I'm beginning to believe we have two planal distortion points here."

"That is very hard to believe, but there's the evidence!"

"One is hard to believe. Two borders on impossible."

"I think only one. That thing is in the one. The other is a smaller portal," Kitti said. "I sense something, a portent. Bernadette does, too. It's why we waited yesterday and today. The time has a lot to do with it, I feel."

"Time?" he looked at the legend on the laptop. "It's four forty nine, December nineteen, two thousand twelve. That's Nola, so we're more east. Three forty nine."

"Two days," she replied.

"To what?"

"The end."

"End of what? You don't make sense."

"That's the big question," Bernadette answered. "The Mayan calendar. It's not supposed to be the end of the world, only the end that will mean a radical difference to the future of civilization, or something. I feel, more and more, that this island is somehow involved."

They discussed it for some time. They couldn't figure what might have happened.

"Well, I still have the rest of my vacation to try to figure something out. I think it would be a good thing to get rid of that thing, but it might not be possible. I imagine more could come, so long as that triangle remains.

"I doubt we could hope to do anything about that. It's not a priority, because getting rid of that could mean we also get rid of the other reality. Our worry is that it's in a place where havoc would break out if it found a way out of it's limits. What if there are thousands of those thing, that they could go anywhere they wanted, here? That's a very scary possibility. It would put us into those stupid BEM movies, for real!

"It's been there for thousands of years, I suppose. Why change it now?"

"According to what I've learned, it's been there for about three hundred years, but it could have been a lot more. There was no one here before that," Bernadette said.

"Not even the Caribbes?"

"I've wondered why they weren't living on this island. It's relatively close to places they settled. It's certainly got everything a primitive society would need! And then some!"

"Shit! I can't go to the elders or whatever to see if there were legends!"

"There are some almost pure Caribbes on Suchando, just fifteen miles from here, by water," Kitti said. "We can go in my boat. Tomorrow at dawn?"

Bernadette grinned. He laughed, and said, "Why the ... heck not!"

The craggy old man, Rosto, tribal elder and historian, of sorts, replied, "We have not gone there since my grandfather seven times removed ruled that there was a hole in the Earth there that swallowed all the people who had lived there since his grandfather, many, many times removed."

"A great evil," Bernadette said. "We know of a great evil there."

"Evil? No. Just not natural, in this place. It is not in its place, there. It only is. It is not evil nor good. It only is. It is not evil to eat a fish, to the fish. It only is. That is natural. That hole is not natural in that place."

They discussed the island. Max figured the trouble there started three hundred ten or twelve years ago.

Kitti suddenly cried, "Three hundred nine years! It moved three hundred nine years ago!"

"What moved?" Bernadette demanded.

"It. What? What did I say? It was a flash.

"Max, what talent I have is like that. I will say something, and not remember it. We call it a flash talent."

"She will tell a fact that is under discussion. Answer a question about it," Bernadette explained. "It seems we know a bit more about the triangle. It moves. We can hope it moves again, but that will probably be in hundreds of years."

"Just so it doesn't leave that thing here when it does!" Max said. "Also, just so it doesn't move to a place with a lot of population!"

They spent a couple of hours on the picturesque island, made a few friends among the Indians, then went back to Hell.

Hell Island. Max felt he really should differentiate that point!

The questions were answered as much as they ever would be, probably. Might as well enjoy a Caribbean Christmas! Back to the grind would come soon enough.

<u>*A Meeting of Friends*</u>

Christmas day, which wasn't celebrated on Hell Island, Bernadette, Kitti, and Max decided to visit the other reality. They started to go toward the eastern path, but Bernadette said she sensed no danger, whatever. Max had proven they could go a shorter path with reasonable safety. The difficult part was cut away on his original trek.

"I feel there is no danger. That it is ... gone?" Bernadette said. "There is no warning sense at any of the branches in the path."

They were standing by the bridge. Max called, "Carey! It's Max and friends! Are you home?"

There was no answer. They crossed the bridge, and Max called again. Nothing. At the cave, there was no sign of Carey. The fire pit hadn't been used for several days, it seemed. Nothing seemed disturbed.

Max went to look into the cave. It was fairly comfortable-looking. Carey was, as not expected, very neat. It didn't seem that anyone had been in the cave in several days.

There was a big piece of cardboard with a series of figures composed of the four upright lines and a slash across. Numbers. Days, Max decided, when he saw the dates above a line. The top date was Dec. 28, 1961. Each year, starting on January 1, headed a line.

2012 had 71 5-markers. That was ten days short of January 1, 2013. December 21. There was a small piece of charcoal Carey had used for a marker. He wrote short notes on the bottom right of the cardboard. The last one said God told him to go to the gold place today. There were several that said the same thing, some saying he was to go to the rock, or to the wailing tree.

He looked around. There was a box with several pounds of gold nuggets. There were other things collected.

Max went back out. "It seems Carey's calendar ended the same day as the Mayan calendar."

Kitti and Bernadette looked at each other. Bernadette said to bring her something personal from Carey. She had little talent to read such things, but she would know if he was alright or in danger.

Max brought a cup with a little coffee in the bottom. Bernadette looked confused. "He is alive ... but is not? It is cold. He cannot stay there, but he dares not go back. He is hiding, but is not in danger from the thing he is hiding from. It no longer exists?

"It is not remotely possible for us to influence anything concerning him."

They decide to leave things as they were, and to go on. Maybe the questions would resolve themselves.

The portal was still there. They spent two days with Octon and Juli. Several others came. It was a very pleasant meeting, then Max, Kitti, and Bernadette headed back to the cabin.

All-in-all, it was a great vacation! Max was convinced that a very few people did have a psy talent, but not in the voodoo vein. There had been a planal distortion that had moved. That theree was a portal on Hell Island to another reality.

That he and Kitti would spend the rest of their lives together in the heaven that was Hell Island.

Halloween 2013

Max grinned at Kitti, who was fixing dinner. They had the laptop on the World News Tonight from Puerto Rico. He had installed a solar panel to charge the batteries and to run a few lights and such around the cabin. They were more than comfortable there was why they didn't live in the states, or somehwere else.

"It was a year ago tonight when we met," Kitti said. "We have lived ten lifetimes since."

"Yes. We belong together. Fate, and all that," Max replied. "That tastes half as good as it smells, I declare you a master chef!" He turned back to the news.

"... the storm passed without much damage.

"Here's a little thing that fits Halloween! A true puzzle, complete with a monster!

"A scientific crew exploring in the Andes, not far from the southern Peru border, has come upon what they first thought was a frozen tree trunk, on the order of the banyan, which is composed of several intertwined trunks. Upon examination, it was discovered that the supposed tree was an animal of some sort. There is nothing remotely like it that has ever been classified. DNA samples indicate it might not be a life form from this planet!

"That is one for the books! A frozen alien in the Andes! I find it hard to credit. It's probably a hoax ... but this is verified! Very strange!

"A note; the body of a man who appeared to be in his eighties was found nearby. He was dressed in shorts and a worn tee shirt. In the Andes! Far above the permanent ice line!

"Well, Brenda! That seems to be a good kind of story to release on Halloween!"

"Yes, it is, Lorna! I would think it was a hoax, like you, if it wasn't that this is authenticated.

"In other news, President Obama, of the United States, has released a program designed to...."

Kitti, who was looking at the screen over his shoulder, said, "I think maybe the triangle has moved to where it won't cause any problems for another three hundred years!"

"We can hope."

A Very Scenic Trap
© 2012 & 2021 by C. D. Moulton

Nancy Ann Gilders had married Harry Silvers after knowing him only eleven days. He was very wealthy, she was comfortable, but not rich.

They spent four years in a very happy marriage. They traveled to many places.

Then he was murdered with a very rare and hard-to-trace poison.

He left a daughter and son and Nancy Ann.

All three had apparently been cleared in the murder. All three became very personally wealthy at his death.

Nancy Ann had to get away. She made plans with the daughter to take a trip.

Then it got scary. Was someone trying to get rid of all three heirs?

Contents

The Funeral

Nancy An n Gilders-Silvers choked back a sob as the casket was slid into the vault.

This was the end of her whirlwind marriage? This was the end of four years of traveling around the world seeing exotic places? This was the end of romantic nights and exciting people?

It wasn't going to be that way. It was the end of Harry's life, but not hers. She was twenty three and Harry had been fifty seven. Everyone said it would not work and that she was only after his money. She had made it plain to the world that she had a very good, if not perfect, marriage and that she had made Harry Silvers happier, as he often said, than any man had a right to be.

She put a hand on the casket and it was placed. The party slowly filed out of the mausoleum.

Francine Dina Silvers, Harry's twenty two year old daughter and Gerald Roland Silvers, Harry's twenty six year old son, joined her at the long black limousine for the ride to the estate. She had gotten along with her stepchildren (even though Gerry was older than she) quite well after the initial suspicion and resentment for taking their deceased mother's place. They were intelligent and realistic people and knew it was psychological and that their father had been a single widower for nine years. It was inevitable that he would someday seek a companion. He could not be expected to spend the rest of his life without companionship. That he was in love with Nancy Ann was obvious and that he was happy was as obvious. That she was not only after his money was shown by the prenuptial agreement that she would get nothing in a divorce or if anything happened to him in the first two years of the marriage. That she had repeatedly stated that it should be a permanent agreement, not one of only a term, but he insisted, saying no wife of Harold Silvers was going to be left destitute if something happened should make it plain to the world that she wasn't a golddigger. She had proven to him in many ways that it was him she wanted, not money.

She choked back another sob. Fran put a hand on her arm and squeezed lightly. Gerry patted her shoulder.

"It's over," Nancy said sadly. "Oh, God! It's over! I can't believe it's over!"

"The last thing Dad would have wanted is for you to let your life stop," Fran said. "He knew he waited too long to let his own continue."

"He was just glad that you were there when he was ready to go on," Gerry said. Nancy patted the hand on her shoulder.

"Now the hard part, if there could be anything harder," Fran said. "We have to live with the fact someone hated him enough to kill him. We have to find out who and why. Someone knows something and the police are doing what they can with what they have.

"I think we should offer a reward, substantial, for information. We might get something. Would you agree to a ten thousand dollar reward?"

"I would agree to a hundred thousand dollar reward!" Nancy cried.

"Let's make it fifty thousand," Gerry suggested. "I knew you'd agree. We have to do something."

"Seventy five and agree," Nancy said.

"We'll do that, then," Fran said. "We can tell Stan to post the reward when he reads the will this afternoon."

Nancy nodded and choked back another sob.

"... evenly among my three main heirs. My wife will receive the large property here in Beverly, my son the horse farm in Napa, and my daughter the San Francisco and Detroit homes. My great love is to be shared evenly among those same three heirs.

"I charge my attorney, Stanley Joshua Levin, with ascertainment that the terms of this will be respected and carried out as tendered.

"I will someday meet all of you again in the place the Lord has prepared.

"Harold Joseph Silvers.

"Are there any questions?"

"We all knew what was in the will," Gerry said. "Dad read it to us just two months ago when he changed it after Gramps died. "We want to post a reward for any information leading to the capture and conviction of the person or persons who murdered Dad."

"You...? Of course. That would be quite the appropriate thing to do. I would suggest five thousand dollars?"

"No," Nancy insisted. "Seventy five thousand dollars is what we agreed."

"*Seventy* ...! That is quite a sum!" Stan cried. "Are you quite sure you wish to offer such a large reward?"

"For God's sake, Stanley! It's only money! We want to find the one who killed our father!" Fran cried.

"I would opt for one million or more. It's not important. This has to be resolved before any of us will find peace," Nancy said.

"Very well. Your wishes will be carried out," Stan said stiffly. "I only ... I think the amount is excessive."

"There isn't any 'excessive.' It's only money. We have far more than we need or want." Nancy said quietly. Fran and Gerry nodded vigorously.

They soon broke up the meeting. Stan left with a check for seventy five thousand dollars to put in a bank account to be used when the terms of the reward were met or in five years, whichever came first. They went home. They got along very well and would stay, for the time being, in the Beverly Hills estate.

The Investigation

Det. Sam Green grunted and dropped the thick file on his desk. "It's a hell of a lot of information that tells us nothing," he complained.

"Let's make a basic fact sheet with what we have," Lt. Cindy Baker suggested. "We have an information overload with that. We could miss the important things because they're mixed in with a hundred unimportant bits."

"We can do a basic chronological-type outline. That's what this is, but it has 'way too much detail.

"Okay. First, he was born in nineteen fifty five, we don't need the parents' background. It was in Markham, Michigan. Went to grammar school and what they called Junior High back then in Markham. They moved to South San Francisco in nineteen sixty nine in the Hippie-Flower Child era. He went to high school in San Mateo.

He started a little tie-dye business in seventy and made a bit more than his father, who was a medical lab technician. In nineteen seventy three he opened a booth in a storefront on Page Street in the city that sold anything popular among the hippies as to clothing. He made more than half a million dollars that year and moved across the bay where he attended Berkeley. He opened a factory there while getting his MA in literature that produced stage equipment for the big rock bands. He earned more than three million in seventy five with various ventures and bought out a number of businesses that were losing their asses. He made a go of all of them. He married Sarah Collins in eighty four and Gerald was born in eighty five. Francine was born in ninety. Sara died of cancer of the ovaries in two oh oh three.

"He didn't have any strong enemies. Actually, he didn't seem to have any enemies at all, which makes me suspicious of some of this. Everybody has *some* enemies, even if they're only mild stuff. Somebody who would maybe get a charge out of knocking you on your ass.

"He married Nancy Ann Gilders in two oh oh eight. They seemed more than ordinarily happy. They traveled a lot. He died of a dose of a rare organic poison this year. We don't know where it came from in any positive sense. It came from Southern Central America because that's where it grows. We don't know for certain how it was administered. It was ingested and is damned fast. Whoever gave it to him was with him because it acted in seconds. It has a lot of cyanide in it. The poison is from the seeds of a plant in *rosacea*, which are the almond family.

"Doctor said he didn't take any medications other than an occasional sleeping aid and vitamin C, small dosage. Acetaminophen, rarely.

"No one we can find any motive for was there. The closest was Gerald, but by only a hundred miles or so. He was in Arizona. Wife was in the Detroit place with daughter. All confirmed.

"Kids, all normal. Close family.

"Nancy Ann Gilders-Silvers, raised in Florida and moved to LA to try to get into modeling for ads. Harold owned two big agencies. One was a talent agency and one an ad producer. She's a looker. She met him at a private party where the producers were meeting the new prospects. It was love at first sight and all of that.

"She's squeaky clean and they were obviously in love. They had a great life together, apparently. They had money and liked all the same things.

"She was a long way from poor when she met him. Not on the same scale, but she was doing very well. She had inherited half a mil and was making on the order of fifty G per year.

"She tends to a certain amount of fat, but we wouldn't notice it, particularly. She wanted to be a model and keeps her weight down. She says you have to set a goal and stay on course to get what you want. Has to be careful of diet for that. No health problems. She's as healthy as Harold was.

"That's what we have. It doesn't give a hint of a direction."

"So. We dig. There has to be something. That seventy five grand reward should bring something out of the woodwork!"

"Yeah! It'll bring us fifty people who know something that's a guess. If they hit it, they get rich quick!" Sam said cynically. "We'll start getting those this morning. The reward notice is in the papers. We have to check them all out."

"There's that."

They wrote down points for each to research. The calls started coming in almost immediately: "Detective? I really shouldn't be calling you because I'm not really positive it wasn't the booze, but Nancy once told me, about a month ago, that she was getting tired of catering to that old man she married and acting like they were getting along so perfectly in public when they weren't in private."

"Okay. Who are you and exactly where did this happen?" Cindy asked.

"I don't think I should give you my name. It was at a party at their house in Beverly Hills. It was on a Saturday just before ... I remember! It was my friend's birthday! March seventeenth!

"How do I collect the reward?"

"First, the information has to lead us to something. This

could be important information. Your code number is forty-forty-five-forty and your key is Cindybaby."

"Okay. How will you contact me?"

"You contact us when the news is released that we've made an arrest. It'll be all over the news. It's a high-profile case."

"Okay."

"Our first reward seeker?" Sam asked.

"Uh-huh. Nancy told her she was thinking of getting rid of her husband at a party at the Silvers home on the night of March seventeen."

"How did she manage that? She was in Madrid on March seventeenth."

"Oh, she hopped a jet and had the party in LA, then got back to Madrid early the next morning or something. We'll get a lot of those, no doubt."

"Uh-huh. That'll be another." The line lit and buzzed.

"Green."

"Detective Green? I'm Carl Ford, not my real name. I'm a druggist in Detroit. I sold Gerald Silvers some special medicines two weeks ago in Detroit. It was under the counter stuff they use for treating internal parasites made from almond oil."

Sam grinned at Cindy. "Internal parasites made from almond oil? What?"

"No. The stuff. Almond oil contains cyanide. This stuff was concentrated and had to be cut with twelve ounces of water to one quarter ounce of the stuff."

"Two weeks ago in Detroit? Can you give an exact date?"

"Yeah. Monday, April thirty. About one thirty in the afternoon."

"I would give you a code for if this is important except for one thing."

"One thing? What?"

"Gerald Silvers was in Napa for the races from the twenty seventh to May two, so he couldn't have been in Detroit."

The line went dead. Sam shook his head.

They got thirty nine more calls. They only had to check four of them. The others were obviously false reports, discovered when the date or time didn't match what could have happened. You can't buy gelatin capsules and ant poison in San Francisco when you're in Miami.

"Well, we'll get more, but very few now," Sam said. "I'll take Moore Street and Colbert Place, you take the two in Carmel."

He went to his car and drove to the herbal shop where a woman reported she had seen Francine buying what might have been poison. A lot of the things there had warnings that they contained various things.

The proprietor said that Francine often bought a few aromatic herbs to make incense. She never bought anything medicinal except hypericin when she couldn't sleep. At least, that one had a small basis.

The one on Moore Street didn't sell anything that was toxic except to people with allergies and wouldn't know the Silvers if they did come in.

Cindy came up with a place with some slight possibility. They had sold ant poison to a number of people. Mrs. Silvers did come in, but usually for hypericin. The other was a phony.

"Well, we can call Doc Danders and see what we have."

Danders said it very likely wasn't ant poison, which was pure sodium cyanide, and it as likely wasn't a derivative from ant poison. It was too specific for that mistake to have been made. There were also trace amounts of a lot of other organic compounds not generally in the diet and that were found in the *rosacea*. They were not found in ant poison.

"Well, that came to a screeching halt! What next?" Cindy asked. Sam shrugged and said book type investigation. "Nose around the area close to that estate, but we won't find anything. I'll go to his business offices. There might be something I can use there. His personal accountant is also his business accountant, so he's there and can give me a few background things."

"Might as well," Cindy replied.

"I'm going to research this *rosacea* bit. There should be some way to find exactly which one we're looking for. If I remember, there are a lot of them. Almonds to peaches. Maybe Doc found something that tells ... he said that this was from Central America. That should mean he can tell us which species it is and we can find who was where it grows or something."

Cindy agreed that might be one approach. It was one more than they had so far.

The Trip Begins

"Nan, we can't sit around here. I'll go nuts! You and Dad were planning that Central American and Caribbean tour. Gerry can handle things here. Seeing the tour is booked, we can just change his name to mine and we can go. It'll be good for both of us. We can't sit here and brood like this! You and I both know full well it's what he would have wanted."

"Oh, Fran! I don't know. I'll miss him so much! I really couldn't!"

"Nonsense! It's what he would have suggested and you know it. I already asked Gerry about it and he said it would be just like Dad to demand it if he'd known."

"Well, it's two more days. I'll say a tentative 'yes' and see how I feel by then. If I'm still in this funk I'll take the chance it will cheer me up some. I'll worry about what people will think, so soon."

"If they knew Dad they'll think it was exactly what he'd want. If they didn't know him, who gives a shit?"

"You do have a point! Maybe I'll seriously consider it!"

The next day she had considered it and decided it really was what Harry would have wanted. That would be just like him. People who knew them would say the same thing to the last one.

They made the flight to Mexico City, where the tour was to begin, by ten minutes. Nancy had raced around at the last minute to change some of the things she would take. Fran had said they were suitable for the funeral, but not for a tour. Nancy had to agree that they were a little too depressing to have along, but she wasn't looking for anybody to show her a good time and didn't want to look like she was on the make.

They stayed two days in Mexico City. It was a fascinating place. Nancy was able to let loose just a little and did have a good time. They saw the St. Albans in a restaurant. Annette told John she won the bet. She knew full well Harry would have made it plain to all of them that they were not to change their plans one degree if anything happened to him. She would have the same agreement. If anything happened to her, Harry and the kids were to do what they had planned together in honor of her memory. She said she had never thought about it, but that was pretty much how she felt.

Guatemala City was picturesque, but Nancy always felt someone was watching her there. The people weren't as friendly as the Mexicans.

Belize was just plain blah.

Honduras and Nicaragua were places she was able to let loose a bit more. She even danced with a handsome Latin Lover type. He was using a standard line and she got a kick out of it. The Smithfields saw them shopping at a street bazar in Managua. They were going back to California from their little hideaway place on the beach (Yeah! fourteen rooms little!). Freida said pretty much what Annette had said.

Costa Rica was a bust. She always felt in danger there. She was about to suggest they leave the tour and meet it again in Panamá City. She didn't like having to stay together with everyone in a group because it was dangerous to be alone. Fran argued that it was only two nights. They could handle that. She reluctantly agreed.

That night at dinner a Tica came to their table and spoke to Nancy, saying she didn't expect to see her in Costa Rica.

"You know her?" Fran asked when she left after a few pleasantries.

"Her sister or aunt or something was a housekeeper for a

man, Frank Genatti, I worked for once five or six years ago. I only met her the once when she was visiting there. I'm amazed that she remembered me!"

They as much as forgot about it.

In the morning there was a note at the hotel desk for Nancy to contact Carmencita Alvarez at a cell number. It was urgent. She stepped outside for privacy and spoke for a few minutes, then came back in to say, "I can't believe the nerve of some people! She wants to borrow money!"

"Aren't you used to that? People have wanted to borrow money from us everywhere we've been," Fran answered.

"Oh, twenty or thirty dollars, I wouldn't mind. I knew her sister a little and I know life can be hard here. She wants five thousand dollars!"

"That is a bit extreme," Fran said, laughing. "Tell her five, okay. Fifty, maybe. Five hundred, not a chance!"

"I wish I'd gone on to Panamá City. I'm feeling trapped here with some crazy nutcase now!"

"Forget it. She'll realize it was a stupid thing to do."

"I hope so!"

They went to take a lot of pictures of all the scenic places. This was billed as a tour for that specific purpose, what they called a "scenic trip to exotic places." It avoided a lot of the tourist trap spots, staying in a larger city at night and using a private bus to go out into the picturesque parts of the countries. When they returned to the hotel Carmencita was waiting there. She said she apologized for her earlier call and really only needed about fifty dollars right now, but decided to start high. It was a stupid thing to do before she explained what was happening with her. She only needed enough to get some new medications and some sleeping pills today. Nancy sighed and gave her thirty five dollars, all she had in cash.

She would get some more cash from the ATM in the morning, but that was all she had now. She said she had a very reliable sleep medicine and gave Carmencita a pill to take just before she went to bed. She'd sleep very well for about eight hours.

They returned to the hotel just before dark and Fran told her the whole group were going to a famous restaurant and night club for the evening. She said she didn't feel at all like going to any nightclub. She was tired and was getting much too depressed for that. She would eat a quiet meal at the hotel and go to bed early with a Xanax. It would snap her out of the mood, she hoped. She still had four of them in the tin. She'd given one to Carmencita.

She went to the tin on the dresser and showed it to Fran. She opened it and said, "That's strange! There were five in it when I took one last night, I carried that one because I might get depressed on the trip, and there are five here. I'm sure when I took one last night there were only five left and I took the one with me. There should only be four."

"Is it important?" Fran asked.

"I don't know! I don't know why there'd be an extra! It was *not* there last night, but was this morning! How did it get there and why was ... oh, my God!"

"Don't take that pill!" Fran demanded. "Dad took a pill ... but ... now I'm getting scared!"

"Oh, God! I wish I'd gone to Panamá City! I wish to *God* I was there right now.

"Maybe ... we were gone all day. Maybe it was put in while we were out. It's more likely. I'm still scared. Now I can't eat anything!"

"Only eat in the restaurant. Don't leave the table for any-thing and then come back to finish what's there. This is something beyond ... I'm not going to the restaurant tonight. I think we should stay close together until I can figure ... something.

"Let's stay together! Neither goes anywhere without the other. Let's go to my room. We *know* someone was in here."

Nancy bit her lip and nodded. They went to the adjoining room and in. Fran went to the bathroom and came back out to find Nancy staring at the dresser with shock and fear on her face.

"What's the matter? Nan! What's the matter?!"

She pointed. There was a candy mint on the water glass tray with a loose wrapper that said, "Compliments of the hotel to our valued guests."

"They don't give mints here. Certainly not ones that have been opened!" she whimpered. "Oh, *God*!"

"Something is very wrong here," Fran said. "Something is definitely out of sync in what we thought. Is someone trying to kill all of ... Gerry!" She grabbed the phone and almost screamed the California number into it. It rang six times and she was about to panic when Gerry answered.

"What's up, Sis?"

"Gerry, someone tried to poison us!" she cried.

"Us? Poison? I don't..."

"I think so. We'll have to have some things analyzed."

"Wait a minute! Someone tried to poison *both* of you?"

"I think so. I'm calming down some now." She explained about the Xanax and the mint. "Gerry, are you sure there's not some way ... I think you have to be careful. Someone is trying to kill all of us for some reason."

"It damned well begins to look that way. Who? Why? It would have to be money, but who gets it if we're all dead?"

She asked Nancy who got her money if she died.

"You and Gerry. I don't have a will."

"I think we should make wills that leave everything to the cancer fund or something. It'll have to be something where none of us profit."

"I'm a hundred fifty percent for that!" Nancy cried.

"Gerry, make up wills that don't leave anything to anyone we know. For all of us. We'll come back and take care of that bit. It should make us safe."

"Done! Get here as fast as you can."

She called the airport and booked a flight in the morning to San Diego. It was the first one that took them close to home, then called the tour and said they had a family emergency and wouldn't be finishing the tour.

She and Nancy slept, what little they could, in the same bed.

In the morning they checked out of the hotel. A police officer was assigned to remain with them until they were aboard the plane. Nancy left fifty dollars at the desk for Carmencita and left the number where she could be reached in California.

When they were aboard the plane Nancy and Fran both sighed a big sigh of relief. Maybe they would live at least long enough to be on home soil!

Fran had some items for the analysis lab at home. The poison used on Harry had come from somewhere in Central America. Costa Rica was in Central America. Harry's poison was, they believed, delivered in a pill. Someone had put it in an acetaminophen gelatin capsule. There were suddenly pills where they shouldn't be here.

This was a long way past merely scary!

Strange Happenings

Gerry was waiting at the gate when they came in. Fran immediately handed him the Xanax and mint.

"Let's go to the estate. I've called the policeman in charge of our case and he'll meet us there. I've had Stan draw up wills that should protect us fairly well. None of us get a dime if one or more of us get knocked off. Nobody but AIDS research gets anything."

They headed back to the estate. Sam Green and Cindy Baker were waiting. Gerry handed Sam the pills. Cindy took them to the cruiser and locked them in the trunk. They then went inside where Sam and Cindy witnessed the wills. When they were signed, Cindy took them and the pills to the station. Word would be out in minutes about the wills. She would return in less than an hour.

Stanley was inside. He had drawn the wills and was introduced to the police when they witnessed the signatures. Gerry said they should be safe enough, but what did it do so far as finding Dad's killer?

"It doesn't make you any safer! Not much!" Stan suddenly cried. "It has to be someone at the companies. The killer will be a partner. Killing you means that the companies will revert to the stockholders. You can't will held stocks to anyone outside because of the way the companies are chartered. Direct heirs inherit. No direct heirs and the stock reverts.

"People, we have a very strange situation here! Fifty three percent of companies worth more than fifteen million dollars revert to the stockholders. There are ten, including you and myself, who are now suspect."

"*We* can't be suspects, surely!" Fran cried.

"You have the estates and about two million apiece. Your two and about a half million apiece in stock value reverts if you die. If you're the only one of us still alive you will gain around ten million dollars in preferred stock."

"Oh, God!" Nancy wailed.

"We have to make some kind of plan where no one gains – but that's not vaguely possible. Even in cases of normal death someone gains," Gerry said defeatedly. "We could possibly sell off our part of the companies to take away the stock inheritance bit. I don't have any other ideas."

"We'll investigate all the control stockholders," Sam suggested. "Most of them will be eliminated because of lack of opportunity. We'll end up with a couple, but that's better than ten."

Hilda, the housekeeper, came to say there was a call from Costa Rica for Mrs. Silvers. Nancy said, "It'll be Carmencita thanking me for the fifty. I'll answer it." She got up and went to the phone on the desk. "Buenos dias, Carmencita! Como estas?"

She listened for a few seconds and slumped almost to the floor. "No! Oh, God, No! *No*! **No**! Oh my God! *No*!"

Fran ran to her. "Nan! What? Snap out of it! Nan! What happened?!" Nancy was shaking and sobbing. Fran took the phone from her and said, "Carmencita?" into it.

"This is Juana, from the Grand Hotel in San José, Costa Rica. I am calling to inform Mrs. Silvers that the woman, Carmencita Alvarez, who Mrs. Silvers left cash for at the desk, was found dead this morning of cyanide poisoning. I wish to know what to do with the money?"

"Keep it! My God! What ... the pill!" She hung up the phone. "Nan! The poison was in the pill you were going to take on the trip! Oh, God! It was supposed to be *you*!"

"Oh, my God!" Nan wailed. "Stan! The money! Give it all to the AIDS thing *now*! Take me off the company! *Now*!"

"No. We can't panic. They failed," Stan said sternly. "We must protect ourselves. We can do it here.

"Nancy, if you are out of the company everyone else is more at risk. I'll issue an emergency order in our names as majority that, should anything more happen to any majority stockholder all company assets will be frozen until resolution of the problem, if you'll order?"

"Yes! Yes! We agree! Do it!" Fran cried. Gerry nodded. Nancy said she would go along with whatever was best and safest for all of them. She had to get away from that place. She didn't know where to go. They even tried to kill her in Costa Rica!

"Dr. Lattimer isn't a stockholder. He was Dad's doctor for years. I'll call him to come. He can give Nan a sedative. We'll work something out. I think the Detroit estate is safest for all of us.

"No! Several of the stockholders live there!"

"Miami," Fran suggested. "It's smaller and, I can't believe I'm talking like this! It's easier to defend."

"I don't have my Xanax. The police ... my God! I'm crazy! I was thinking how I wish I had that *poison* to ... I'm going crazy!" Nan mumbled.

"I think there was only one poisoned Xanax," Fran said. "You said it was added right there at the hotel, so the others will probably be alright."

"No!" Cindy ordered. "You are not to take any medication of any type that is in this house or any other of your houses at this time! It is all too possible that your father's death was because one pill among those he had was poisoned. The killer could depend on his taking it at some time.

"Sam, I think we should test everything in this house that could be used. There could be more."

"Oh, God!" Nancy cried. "If there's anything like that we'll all get it, sooner or later! There's no hope!"

"No," Sam said quietly. "If it's something here now, you're safe. Nothing here now will ever be taken. Period. You have to ascertain that anything you take in the future is from something you bought right then. Shop in random pharmacies. Buy candies and such from a public counter. No special orders that could be delivered with an added ingredient. Use logic and common sense and you should be safe that way. You're lucky that poisoners don't graduate to guns."

"Graduate to...?" Fran asked, then nodded.

"This situation gets stranger and stranger. We have to figure it out and *stop* it!" Cindy agreed.

Sam got a call on the radio he carried. There was poison in the mint, but not in the Xanax.

"It was added right there at the hotel. The killer was there!" Gerry cried.

"Or a hired hand was," Cindy said cynically. "Sam, we have to find which contract killer was in Costa Rica, I think. We can trace back."

"It's a break, if a strange one!" Sam agreed.

<u>*A Question*</u>

"What do we have?" Sam asked Cindy back at the station. "Other than a lot of questions, that is."

"We have an equation with missing parts and parts that are from some other equation."

"That one missed! It doesn't make sense!"

"Neither does this case."

"You have a point. I've got the word out to look for any possible suspected contract killer from here, Michigan, Florida, Oregon or Texas who could have been in Costa Rica."

"Oregon?"

"Harvey and Janet Billings are there."

"And?"

"They have six percent of the control stock."

"Oh."

"I have a question."

"*One*?!"

He grinned and gave her the finger salute. "Why does so much of this mess seem contrived? I've watched everyone we've been in contact with and they're dead on the money, please excuse the expression, as to acting within their personalities.

"Why does it seem so contrived?"

"I know what you mean. Every single one of them is acting too perfectly, according to profile."

"I think I want to get into the education of each of them. It's too good to not be practiced."

"One of them is a hell of an actor."

"Cindy, it could be more than one."

"Brother-sister team? I personally doubt that!"

"Or lawyer and any one of them."

"You don't like lawyers."

"Who does? Beside the point.

"We have to concentrate on the suspects there at the estate today. They're the ones who could gain anything by an act. Joe Blow in Schenectady would be wasting his time putting on an act. We wouldn't see it."

"But we did see that bunch. I like all of them. I hope we're wrong."

"Me too – but we're not."

"I'll check on the Mrs. and the lawyer, you check on the brother and sister, okay?"

Sam sighed. "Okay."

Sam went to the files to study what they had on Francine Leslie Silvers and brother Gerald Arthur Silvers. They both had earned advanced degrees in business administration. Gerald also had taken classes in psychology (bingo?) and some science courses. Basic chemistry and physics. He did well in business and psychology and not so well in science.

Francine had also taken some psychology and accounting. She did well in all of it. With both of them taking psychology the bingo was pointless unless they were co-conspirators. Francine was taking post grad courses, probably going for a phd.

While he was at it: they both did well in grade schools. Gerry did well in athletics and probably could have gotten a scholarship for either baseball or football. There was a note that the father said athletics weren't part of business and ended any such opportunity. That probably explained the psychology courses. Business, particularly in advertising, used psychology extensively.

Post schooling: perfectly normal.

There was nothing there except the psychology. That applied to both. It wasn't high on his list of background poisoning anymore, it was only there because of what could be a practiced act. So far as Det. Samuel Green was concerned, it was both or neither.

Four hours and he had what he was going to find. How was Cindy doing?

Cindy first checked the lawyer, Stanley Morris Levin. He was successful and had the schooling and courses most lawyers had. He had studied psychology, but any lawyer worth a bent penny in court had to know some. It was how to reach a jury. His court record was excellent. He practiced mostly business and civil law, concentrating 80% on corporate.

He was never a suspect in anything, so far as Cindy Baker was concerned. Sam was the one who couldn't bring himself to trust any lawyer, but he had years of dealing with them that Cindy didn't have. She didn't trust defense lawyers, but they were a different breed from corporate. Levin didn't have any ethic complaints against him. That was the one area corporate lawyers seemed to be weak in, in her mind.

She ruled him out, thus ruled out conspiracy with any of the others automatically. If there was a conspiracy it was Gerry and Francine, which she didn't believe for a picosecond. Opposite of what she generally felt about such things, she felt maybe Francine was capable, but not Gerry. It simply wasn't in him.

Unless he was a superb actor.

Nancy Ann Gilders Silvers. She read over the basic school records, then went into the details. It seemed she was always pretty, but had shunned running for prom queen or any of that, saying it was pure vanity, and she was never a vain person. She had to work hard to look presentable, but said often that one must set a goal in life and must always aim for that goal. Her goal was to live a good and comfortable life and to travel and see the world. "Station" and "Class" that her mother considered so important were silly to her. She said only the same kind of empty people were impressed, so it really wasn't worth the effort.

Cindy remembered that she had said she had trouble keeping her weight down, but she wanted to be a model and aimed for that. Whatever it took. Waver and lose.

That was a psychological point. Did the end justify the means?

She was Jewish. Cindy looked up what was known about her politics, but she wasn't involved or very much interested in Israel. She did state several times emphatically that she was not a Zionist and thought they were extreme and would never be accepted by the rest of the world. Yes, Israel was in a difficult position in world politics, but much of that was because of the Zionists' inflexible position. Compromise in politics was and always would be what politics was about.

That didn't say much. Nancy could or couldn't believe in the end justifying the means. Cindy read it as meaning that it was always situational. Too often it was situational depending on who the situation benefitted.

She liked Nancy. Nancy seemed to be a sincere person whose life was disrupted by this. She had plenty. She didn't seem to want millions, just to be comfortable.

There was nothing in her education that said much. She had studied independently, mostly using the internet. She had a very wide range of interests. She liked to travel and managed to fit in wherever she was.

The doctor's reports on her and Levin showed very little problem. There was a note that she was probably unable to ever bear children, which had depressed her for a very short time, but she had accepted it as one of the bad things life visits on people. It seemed she never let anything negative bother her for any length of time. She had broken down at the death of her mother, but was back to normal in less than ten days.

She feels the emotional things intensely, then passes on. Good trait to have! Cindy thought.

There wasn't much here. She hoped Sam had come up with something.

"Not much. No sudden insight that solves the case. No convictions for poisoning or anything else. Normal people in a way and abnormal in another," Sam reported.

"Normal but abnormal?"

"They're all the good friend you meet on a night on the town and the type you giggle and confide your dark inner secrets with. That's abnormal in the level of society they happen to inhabit."

Cindy nodded slowly. "They're able to blend in with wherever they are and whoever they're with. That's the one question I have about the way they relate and the way others relate to them. Nancy's the only one raised at that level. High end, but barely inside that level.

"Sam, they're chamaeleons. Every one of them. That makes it impossible to get a true perspective on any of them."

"Chamaeleons. That's a good description, but it's not a negative thing in this case."

"No. It's an ability I wish I could cultivate. It could make life a lot less complicated."

"It could also give you an uncanny ability to hide. A survival trait."

Cindy nodded.

Where and When?

"Let's get together and see if maybe we can find something," Gerry suggested. "The police don't know these people, we do. I guess we've all had little theories and that, mine at least, are already knocked out of the running.

"We're missing something. It may be a matter of a place or time when we either saw or heard something that didn't register. There has to be that one clue that's there that we're overlooking.

"Where did something happen? When? How? What is it that we probably all know that tells us who's trying to knock all of us off?

"I can't believe it's a stockholder with a crazy scheme to take control of the companies. Trouble being, I can't think of anything else. Anything else would have to be revenge for something."

"I think it may be envy," Nancy suggested. "Some nut is killing us because we have a lot and they have nothing. Or something."

"They have something," Fran said. "They can hire a killer or can travel all over after us."

"We just have to be damned sure we've covered everything," Nancy replied. "If there was a slip somewhere we have to find it and deal with it."

"We have to be able to find it with solid enough certainty that we're convinced," Fran said. "If it's some little thing the police can't act on because of some silly technicality I'm about ready to hire my own killer. The trouble with that is I wouldn't have a clue as to how to find one."

"According to TV, you find some bodybuilder jerk with a

three-day beard and a thousand dollar suit and a tough guy attitude," Gerry replied. "They hang around bars with a lot of strippers and hoods around.

"I've met a hood or two. They were angling to get into Dad's businesses. That was a brick wall! Dad would ruin them if he could. Remember that Gino Banderi or something such? Dad had him running back to Sicily, fast, or he'd face extortion charges even he couldn't get around. Dad had recorded the whole thing. Dad had all that advert studio stuff installed in his office."

"You don't suppose...?" Fran said, thinking. "He could have someone among the stockholders to end up with all of it."

"And the first time his ugly face showed up anywhere where there was anything to do with the companies he'd be gone!" Gerry said. "I wondered about that from the first. It could be another of them, though. It's far-out, but those things can happen. I guess. Maybe. I'll ask Sam about that."

"They definitely use contract killers," Nancy argued. "Sam would find them in a heartbeat. We can hope that's it because it would be finished fairly fast. I think, if it's someone you would call professional and if he was after all of us Gerry would have gotten something, and he wasn't, so it's not all that professional. They'd go after all of us at once or not at all."

"We don't know there wasn't something for Gerry," Fran cautioned. "If not, I'd tend to agree with that one."

"I can't think of anything. Harry and I never met anyone who seemed to have anything against him for any reason," Nancy said. "It has to be because we're rich or for the companies, somehow. That's all that figures."

"One thing occurred to me," Fran said. "Those conspiracy people."

"Conspiracy people? That global banking and control the economy conspiracy? We're not any part of that! We aren't related to any of those super-rich people!" Fran cried.

"No. We're just a family of rich Jews," Gerry said. "To them, it's the same thing. I wish you hadn't brought that up. There are thousands of them!"

"I think they'd want to gloat, to try to scare the so-called conspirers," Nancy argued. "They would already be saying that killing Harry showed the world we aren't immune to them. I don't think that's it.

"I don't think the possibility should be ignored, either."

They all agreed with that.

"I think I'll call Sam and ask him about the likelihood of the mafia or conspiracy theorists," Gerry suggested. "It certainly wouldn't hurt anything." He took the phone and called. Sam said he hadn't thought of that, but Cindy had. He was a Jew and the gentile thought of something so obvious! It was, as usual with them as a group, on speaker.

"Oh, and one other thing that adds to the mob part. We discussed that. If it was a professional hit man he would try to get you all at once. That would include the mob.

"We found cyanide in a Snickers bar in the desk. Would that be for you, Gerry?"

"It would have to be. I'm the only one who eats chocolate. I'm not watching my waistline. So it was professional."

"True that it *appears* to be professional. I'm not altogether convinced for one other reason."

"What's that?"

"There was no one in Costa Rica who was ever even suspected of being a hit man while Nancy and Fran were there."

Nancy inserted, "I've been thinking. You keep saying hit

man, but isn't poison almost always a woman's method?"

"The term's inclusive. I'll admit I didn't think of that, but the search is always inclusive. There *are* professional hit *women*, too. I've never heard of a hit man using poison in any such fashion. They might poison a whole family, but at some big function where they'd be sure to get them all at once. With cyanide, it'd be a cylinder of the gas in a closed room or something, or ricen on a cane tip or such for just one."

They talked a bit longer about the case, but nothing more was learned. Gerry finally cut the connection. "Back to square one-half," he said bitterly.

"There has to be something somewhere!" Fran insisted. "There's no such thing as the perfect murder!"

"No, but there are a hell of a lot of undetected murders and people who get away with it!" Gerry said.

"Oh, God! We'll have to spend the rest of our lives looking in dark corners!" Nancy said. They all looked worried at that declaration.

Background Noise

"We've got to get something to at least give us a direction," Sam complained. "Our dead ends are our case."

"Sam, I want Ellie Jenkins to go through every computer any of them used. Whoever's behind this had to have some contact of some sort." Ellie was the department's computer expert. "Do you think they'll object?"

"I would want to know why! Good point!" He grabbed the interphone and called Ellie. She said to have Capt. Forbes authorize and she'd be in the car, waiting. She was getting a chronic case of boredomitis.

He called the captain and had the authorization five minutes later. Cindy would take her to the estate to ask permission. Sam would be ready to have a warrant delivered if there was any trouble.

Cindy called on the way and Fran said to come on over. Anything they could find would be a help.

"Should I delete my diary?"

"Ellie will be the only one to see it, but I'd delete it fast if I made plans to poison people in it!" Cindy replied.

"Oh, damn! Could you delay getting here for fifteen minutes?" They laughed and chatted until they were in the long drive. Fran thanked her for giving her the first opportunity to laugh about anything in a week.

There was a desktop and a laptop on the desk when they went into the study. Fran said she brought her personal computer in so they could check. It was too possible it was someone who was in touch with her, though she didn't use it much.

Ellie picked it up and put it to the side. She flipped on the desktop and immediately put her hand behind it. Fran asked what for.

"You don't check to see the fan's running? You could burn it out if the fan stops. One second that can save a five hundred dollar repair."

"I remember that sometimes," Gerry said. "It's something we should all do.

"Should I bring my laptop?"

"Probably a good idea," Ellie said, looking at the screen. She went to the history and scanned the uses. There wasn't much. They didn't use that machine except for office stuff. It had an e-mail she asked if they knew the password or if it was Harry's.

"Harry's. He probably wrote it down somewhere – if we can find it," Nancy said.

"I can get it, "Ellie said. "I'll check to see if there's any-thing he kept there that means anything, but there won't be anything on this machine."

"Should I bring my laptop?" Nancy asked, then, "Stupid! I'd be the most likely one someone made a threat to or something!" She went out.

Ellie went to the e-mail carrier and theharry_ beast12 came in the log-in box. She clicked on "forgot password?" and got a message that a password reset address would be sent to the alternate e-mail. There wasn't any in the recent history so she went to the older history and found a hotmail account. She went to hotmail and both the password and user name were in the box. She said, "Whew!" and logged in. There were several hundred ads and a new message for resetting a password on Yahoo! She went to the address and reset the password to policeinvellie1 and was immediately logged in. She went through the e-mails and said there didn't seem to be anything there. She turned off the machine and looked at Gerry, who said his e-mail, contrary to all advice, was always logged in from that computer.

"Let's go somewhere else while Ellie reads all the horrible things you say about each other in e-mails," Cindy suggested with a laugh. Fran said there were personal things there, but not in the e-mails. "I'll give you the passwords and the password to log onto my locked part of the hard drive." She wrote something on a slip of paper and handed it to Ellie, who promised to use it and tear it up to where no one could read it. Nancy gave her a slip with the same information and they all went into the atrium for iced tea – that Fran bought in the supermarket today. The girl brought a bowl of sugar and some lemon juice.

"Uh-oh!" Gerry said.

"New. Today. One pound sack and one fresh lemon to squeeze. The milk and eggs and so forth are from this morning. I'll go shopping in a different store every day until this is finished!" Fran promised.

They chatted for more than two hours until Ellie said she had found what was there. She would have to get the warrants for the bunch of them and would be back soon! Don't take any sudden trips out of the country! They all laughed.

Cindy said they'd better get back to the office. Thanks. They left.

In the car Cindy asked what that was about, the fan on the computer.

"You noticed how I picked up the laptop, too. If the machines had been used in the past few minutes I would have felt the heat. None of them were."

"Did you find anything?"

"I don't know. There wasn't anything in e-mail or diaries or any of that, which is exactly what I expected. The history on the laptops only keeps a list of the last ten sites in the window. Most people don't know you have to go to DOS to erase them totally. None of them had that was obvious. I didn't go to any of the sites, but listed them all."

Cindy nodded. They drove onto the side lot and parked, then went inside. Sam was talking to a dark young woman he introduced as Carmencita Alvarez's sister, Sylvia Gortas.

"She wants to know what happened to her sister in Costa Rica. I called her about it at the number on Carmencita's cell phone speed dial. What she says is interesting, but may not be important."

"Which is what?" Cindy asked.

"Well, her sister was into blackmail, for one thing."

"Blackmail?"

"Si. She ees for finding things and no say nada for money. No money, she say things."

"So that may be what the five thousand was about?" Cindy asked. "She didn't get it. She got fifty. Eighty five, of which she got thirty five."

"Entonces she no say nada, so es maybe not the something serioso, I think. Si es with proving thing she no take no thirty five for nada!"

"She just wants to know what happened. She says the family knew that somebody would kill her sooner or later, they thought break her neck or carve her up with a machete," Sam said. "By itself, it doesn't mean anything."

"We can hope that something on the computers will connect a couple of things," Cindy said. "Ellie found a long list of things that most people wouldn't know are still on the hard drive or something. I won't pretend I know what she's talking about. Web sites and history."

"Every site they ever visited is on their personal computers. I made them think all I could do was check e-mails and what's on the computer now. Every site is on the lists. G. is Gerald, F. is Fran, N is Nancy, H. is Harry.

"I'll get back to boredom city now. Thanks for the break!" She waved and left. Sam promised they would keep Sylvia informed and she left.

"Well? Ellie kept talking about lists. Where are they?"

Cindy held up a memory stick. "Here. It would be pages on paper."

She inserted the stick into a USB port and clicked on "Open and view files" and the H. and F. and N. etc came onscreen. She clicked on H. and got: CopdXinfserv.com/1450

>INF CDX1450>ink>inserting> cleaning heads >cleaning platten.

>INF CDX1450> ink>refill

Next was PolVce.com/issues

>Forum bcktlk>political>NAFTA

It went on for twenty seven sites having to do with the businesses and politics.

She clicked on G. and got: NCRB>editorial comment

>Egypt>riots

>Rusplncrsh>blame>flight control

and so forth for six pages. They read all sites and wrote down:

WRLDMEDUC>CA>parasites

WRLDMEDUC>rosacea>prunus armenica

MBG>rosacea>prunus armenica

"That's what Doc mentioned. Rosacea," Sam reminded. Cindy nodded and looked grim.

F. had hundreds of sites, mostly chat rooms and such.

N. had hundreds of sites, many about diet and medicine. A

lot about new fashions. A lot about travel. Sam noted that the dates and times of the others were consistent, but there were large gaps in this. How to explain it?

Cindy considered and said she may have an answer for that. She called Nancy and asked if she took her laptop with her on trips.

"Sometimes. Sometimes no. I mean, the ships on most of the ocean cruises have rooms full of computers to use. Why take a laptop and have it stolen?"

She hung up and called Ellie to come explain something. When she was there Cindy asked if it was possible to selectively erase that history.

"Of course. Select and delete whichever you want."

Sam explained that there were gaps, but that Nancy had claimed she didn't take the laptop on some of their cruises.

"How can we tell if that was what happened here?" Cindy asked. Ellie shrugged and said that particular brand didn't have dated erasures in the DOS files.

"I know!" Cindy suddenly cried and went to the computer to read the visited sites. "What?" Sam asked.

"She used Vacation Paradise Fantasies to book their tours."

"It doesn't give dates," Sam pointed out.

She looked up the phone number of the agency and called, talked a few minutes, then said, "Come on! Thanks, Ellie," Ellie went back to her office. She and Sam got a cruiser and went to an address on East Paloma. They went inside where Cindy said she was to speak with a Mrs. Martin?

"I'm Mary Martin, just not the famous one," she said. "You're the police. Silvers?"

Yes. All we need is the tours and dates. We're investigating his death, you know. He may have met someone on one of the tours who can give us some insights."

She nodded and handed Cindy the file laying on the desk. "I made copies. You can take them and I'll keep the originals." They agreed to that and soon left.

Back at the office they brought up the list and noted the dates that were missing. They matched those to the agency records.

"Three times when she might have had repeated visitations to sites we don't know about. The fact they were erased means she had some reason to erase them," Cindy said.

"It might not mean much. Maybe she was trying to free space."

"Then she would have erased these hundreds of things with no significance above and below."

Sam nodded. "We have to know if she had ever visited ... what if she used another computer to find the original sites?"

"Another computer?"

"If she just wanted to find where to look and not spend any time there in series she ... why would Gerry be looking up rosacea?"

"I see. She distilled her own, or whatever they do?"

"No. You can't heat cyanide compounds that way. It decomposes them. What she wanted was to see what she had to add to ant poison to make it appear to be concentrated cyanide taken from rosacea."

"I see. Ant poison with some almond flakes or whatever. A little bit of almond oil.

"I was thinking about that Xanax tablet. It was a little tiny thing. I doubt that much pure cyanide would kill anyone. I would like to see the tablet she gave Carmencita. Want to bet it was a large capsule instead of a tiny pill?

"What did Carmencita know?"

Sam thought and got a smirk on his face. He called a

number and asked to speak with Sylvia Gortas.

"Sylvia? Sam Green here. I have to ask you a question. When did Nancy Silvers come to your offices to meet Carmencita?"

"Carmencita, she is here in Marzo. Seis a la doce."

"What business is Frank Genatti in?"

"We are in the frutas and vegetales importing."

"You import fruits and vegetable for the food market here?"

"Si. And for the medicinas a lot."

"Nancy worked for Genatti at one time?"

"Only for the advertisments. She made the one for the TV. Cure escabiosis with natural producto made with prunus seeds. It is safe, although it have the cyanide."

"Thank you. Would you have a copy of that advertisement?"

"Si. I make copy and send to computadora de policia."

"Mil gracias." He hung up.

"So!" from Cindy.

"Yeah. So."

And the Emmy Goes to...

"Yes?" Gerry said, answering the phone. Sam's ID was on the caller ID screen.

"Gerry? Sam Green here. Are all of you there at the moment?"

"Yes. We don't go anywhere."

"I've learned a few things and want to get some answers about times and places, mostly. We're finally making some progress."

"You're making progress? Thank God!" Nancy said. "Anything to relieve the stress. I can't take much more of this tension."

"Yes. We have a detail from San Bernadino, one from Mexico City, something from Detroit. It all comes together in a definite pattern."

"San Bernadino and Mexico City? I can see Mexico City, but San Bernadino?" Nancy asked.

"It's sometimes very strange how a puzzle that looks like one thing in pieces will form a definite picture of something else when the pieces are in order. You get a lot of pieces that don't seem even part of the puzzle until you suddenly find they were the key to solving the whole thing.

"Can we come over this evening? Say six or six thirty?"

"Anytime!" Gerry answered. He rang off.

"I ask the same question. San Bernadino? It's never come up in this at all!" Cindy remarked.

"Nobody noticed except one. Whether there's something from San Bernadino or not can only matter to one."

"Okay. Why pick San Bernadino?"

"They raise a lot of peaches and apricots there."

"And"

"*Prunus armenica* is an apricot."

She shook her head. No need to go on with this. She'd never know what it was about.

Sam said that because he'd looked up *Prunus armeniaca,* found it was apricot, and had seen the San Bernadino on the label of a box of them in the supermarket.

"We can get a few things together. We can see who's the best actor in this. I want to study some things about her closer before we go over there. I think we'll find she was basically a personality type with a small modification. They're very convincing and persuasive. It's a natural defense mechanism."

"So you've recently started to study for your degree in psychology?"

"Psychological inferiors. Sociopaths. They can be the most charming people you'll ever meet. They can convince you of anything. They project emotions. They don't feel them."

She nodded. She'd read about them in a couple of cases written up by a very famous criminal prosecutor.

"I'm going to relax and put this together in a way that seems damning, though I won't have anymore than I've got now. Fifty circumstantial, no solid."

"Okay. Here? Five thirty?" He nodded.

He was walking out and stopped, said, "I'll buzz out there," and went on out. Cindy shook her head.

"Okay. I have a lot of things in this box," Sam instructed as they drove up the drive to the estate house. "It's actually what convinces me, but it's not enough for a jury. Not by a long shot."

"It would get a jury conviction if we could hope for an

intelligent jury who would look at what's there and not what some defense lawyer says is or isn't there."

"When they can refuse jurors. Yeah."

"I think I can make her admit to a little too much, Cindy. She's thought she's way ahead of us all along. I shook holy hell out of her with San Bernadino.

"Those people don't feel much except a small bit of personal fear. Because they're used to feeling nothing, that little twinge of fear is magnified, but only for a short time. I have to use that time and I need some luck.

"The worst it can do is make Gerry and Fran aware of where they stand with her."

"I'll be damned! I think you got to her a lot more than you thought!" Cindy said, pointing at Stan Levin's big black Mercedes sitting in front of the door.

"As they've said, repeatedly, thank God!"

"They say 'Oh God!' You can use that one, can't you? She has to explain to him why he's here."

"Unless it has nothing to do with her calling him. He is, after all, her lawyer. He might be here to deliver copies of the will or company papers or anything else."

"She'll use that somehow if it's true or not."

"I might be able to use it, anyhow."

"In what way?"

"He's their lawyer, not just hers."

Cindy looked thoughtful as they carried the box inside to sit it on the big desk in the den. Gerry greeted them and said, "Got the conviction papers in there?"

"Yep!" Cindy said. He half grinned and looked questioningly at her, then at Sam.

"We all miss details. There's always a path, it's just that we sometimes can't see it. Sometimes we see it and don't believe it or don't *want* to believe it, as in this case," Sam explained.

"I don't like the sound of that, even a little bit!" Fran said. "Does it mean one of us is the killer?"

"It means ... that. Yes. Can we take a seat or something so I can lay this one out for you?

"Stan, I can see this turning into a problem for you. You're all their lawyer, not just one or two. Representing one will be pitting you against two. You can't avoid a question of conflict of interest I'm afraid."

"No. I represent a corporate entity. I'm not a qualified criminal lawyer. I can give advice to the point of telling them not to answer any questions before they have counsel with experience in such matters. I'll decide which course to follow as this progresses. If I feel possible conflict I will withdraw from counsel because of the conflict of interest clause."

Sam nodded and sat on the edge of the desk.

"Well, we might as well get this over with as quickly as possible. You've been under tension long enough.

"First, let me say I personally like all of you. Cindy feels the same. You're basically very good people, but one of you has a flaw. It's probably a genetic flaw that gives you a different set of priorities and a different moral sense. In short, a sociopath.

"A sociopath doesn't feel much, but can project feelings very well. It's a survival trait. While I have to work at convincing you I'm something I'm not, this person is automatically believable.

"These people sometimes, because they feel so little, set a course to accomplish a thing and are not deterred by mere moral or ethical reasons."

Everyone looked at Nancy, who merely seemed interested.

"I have eight points to show. Now, how do I prove it?"

"Prove what?" Nancy asked.

"That you killed Harold Silvers."

She still seemed interested. "You could only prove that if it were true." It was stated with a slightly hardened voice and posture.

"Gerry, why did you recently research *Prunus armeniaca*?"

"Prunus what? I don't even know what you're talk ... oh. The stuff that killed Dad and that was in my candy bar and the candy mint and Nancy's Xanax."

"Do you let anyone else use your computer?"

"It's on the mantle most of the time. Anyone can use it."

"Oh, the Xanax didn't contain anything but Xanax. That tiny pill couldn't more than make anyone a little sick if it was pure cyanide," Cindy said and brightened. "Fran, how big was the pill Nancy gave Carmencita?"

"The pill? I didn't see ... I think ... I thought it was acetaminophen. It was ... the same kind of thing that killed Dad, huh?

"I sort of noted it in the hotel when she showed me the Xanax. It just missed registering that the pill she gave the woman was a lot bigger. She went on about there being an extra one and I was distracted from that. When she found the mint in my room – that she put there, huh? – it went ten miles from my mind."

"You didn't see the *Xanax* I gave Carmencita!"

"You took it out of your purse when you went out to her. It was in that little bottle thing."

Nancy looked thoughtful. She didn't say anything more.

"Whatever, that's just one in a list of clues," Sam continued. "Harry died of cyanide that was thought to be from *Prunus armeniaca*. It would have to be concentrated to the point a very large capsule would have to be used to deliver it. No such capsule was used. The one used would have to have a super-concentrate, such as the sodium cyanide used in some ant poisons." He took a cannister from the box. "Such as the type you bought at Marviloso Herbals and Pharmacy."

Nancy stared at the cannister like she was trying to will it to disappear.

"Use ninety nine percent this and a little apricot seed in almond oil and analysis would seem to indicate *Prunus armeniaca.*

"If you'd stopped with Harry you would have gotten away with it. Why did you keep going? You wanted it all, not just a few million?"

Nancy shook her head.

"We thought it had to be her," Fran said. "We couldn't understand it. She was awfully good. We thought she really did love Dad.

"Gerry and I arranged for her to go on the tour as a trap. We didn't know you could do that with the ant poison and some stuff from an apricot seed and thought she got the stuff when she and Dad came through Central America two months ago on their way to Bogota. The way she acted in Guatemala City made me think she got it there, but nothing happened and no one met her or anything. I thought the way she acted in Costa Rica might mean something, but she didn't see anyone there out of the ordinary. She just kept wanting to get to Panamá City right away. She made excuses about it, saying she was scared in Costa Rica. I thought we would definitely meet someone there, then the thing about the Xanax. That scared me and, when she found that mint in the hotel room, I got scared and thought we were wrong about her. Someone was trying to kill us all!"

"We set that tour up," Gerry said. "We called it a scenic

trap. Play on words from scenic trip."

"Well, the trap worked, but not the way you thought it would," Cindy said.

"Worked how?" Nancy asked sourly. "All of this is bullshit! It doesn't prove a thing!"

"Sure it does!" Cindy replied. "You did meet the person who would expose you! Carmencita!"

"Bullshit! She was just some nutty woman whose sister I once knew, right! Got it?"

"Yes," Sam answered. "We got it. We got the sister and we got a copy of the advertisement you made for her boss. An advertisement that said a natural cure for scabies was found in the seeds of *Prunus armeniaca*, but you had to be careful taking it because it contained cyanide.

"It's true, you know. Not one of the facts we found means much. When you add them together they mean everything. Any one without the others was speculation. Any one thing could mean two different things. Added together ... two and two is four. Period."

"It is a circumstantial case," Stan said. Sam could have committed a murder at that moment himself! "We have a formula in law concerning circumstantial cases. Three or four such items can be gotten around easily. Five or six can sometimes be gotten around. More than six, plead guilty! You're gone!

"I am a corporate attorney. I am not competent to pursue criminal defense. I must suggest that Mrs. Silvers obtain competent counsel. I must refuse advice due to that factor." He sat down.

"Shit!" Nancy said, almost without any emotion at all.

"What?" Cindy asked.

"I thought I'd feel an emotional rush if you caught me or

something. Adrenalin rush. I don't feel a thing.

"Fran, Gerry, I really did fall in love with Harry. It scared me. I had the plan to get the money, so I just ... kept on.

"Are you going to arrest me now? I promise not to run. I'm through running. I never get anywhere with it."

"I'll be damned! Just like that?" Gerry cried.

"Just like that," Sam and Cindy said together.

Under the Circumstances

"... pled guilty to premeditated murder under impaired mental circumstances. The court finds partial verity in that, but it was a lifelong and genetic impairment that didn't affect the knowledge of right and wrong. It merely rendered you not caring about right and wrong.

"Court therefore finds you guilty as charged and imposes a sentence of twenty years incarceration. Such sentence is not so much punitive as for the protection of society and individuals. You are quite capable of deciding that right and wrong are of no consequence when you plan the murder of the next victim or group of victims.

"Bailiff, take the defendant into custody. So ordered. Court dismissed."

Judge Hanrady gathered her robes and left the courtroom as the bailiff went toward Nancy. She hugged her lawyer and thanked him, waved at Sam, Cindy and her stepchildren and pointed to the door.

Sam shook his head, Cindy grinned, Fran looked questioningly at Sam and Gerry shrugged. They went out the courtroom door and to the right to the holding cell where Nancy and her lawyer were waiting. The lawyer said he had advised Nancy against this.

"Bullshit!" Nancy said with a wave of her hand. "Kids, Sam and Cindy, I feel like an idiot to say something like this, but no hard feelings, okay? I really don't feel anything. About anything. I felt love for your father and it scared the holy living shit out of me. I knew he could control me while I knew he wouldn't. I was confused for a couple of days, then went right back to the original plan. I was going to get all that money and go places and do things, mainly try to find something that really did interest me.

"Kids, I killed Harry because I loved him and I can't take feelings. I spend my whole life trying to feel something, then I do and I want it to stop!

"I planned to get the money I'd gotten. I might as well try to get it all. It was a game. I lost.

"That's about all there is to it. It's like the old Peggy Lee song. *Is That All There Is?*

"I guess I'll just keep dancing. I wish you all the best.

"Any questions, I'll try to answer."

"One," Gerry said.

"What?"

"Who in *hell* is Peggy Lee?"

C. D. Moulton´s works are available on most major outlets as printed or e-books. CD writes the CD Grimes, PI mysteries, the Det. Lt. Nick Storie mysteries, the Clint Faraday mysteries, the Flight of the Maita science fiction series, books on orchid culture and many others of many types. Mystery, adventure, intrigue, science fiction, fantasy, paranormal, mild erotica, and factual.